New Hire

Firehouse Blues Series: Book 8

AE Moran

The Invisible Publishing Company

Firehouse Blues Series

Contents

Chapter 1: Caleb

I pass the hose back and forth across the concrete to wash the soap off the firehouse driveway. I cut off the spray when I see an absolutely drop-dead gorgeous blonde walk down the sidewalk coming from the right.

I whistle at her and she bursts into a big blushing smile. She wears her hair in a wavy ponytail perched high on the back of her head.

Her apple cheeks color and her crystal blue eyes twinkle when she laughs. She's wearing a thick padded jacket, but her pants hug muscular, shapely thighs and a nicely rounded ass. She must have one hell of a body under those clothes.

I stand there not even trying to hide how badly I'm checking her out. She notices and keeps right on blushing. Damn. I don't see women as stunning as her very often.

I wait for her to pass, but instead, she turns into the driveway and comes straight toward me. I find myself grinning back at her. "Hello, good-looking!" I greet her. "Where have you been all my life?"

She laughs again. "Very funny. I'm here to see Fire Chief Broebeck."

I try to make a joke about it. "Don't break my heart. You really came here to see me, didn't you?"

She sticks out her hand. "I'm Allison Metcalfe."

I struggle to shift the hose to my other hand and wipe my wet palm on my uniform pants so I can shake her hand.

"I'm Caleb Watts—at your service." I take a chance and kiss the back of her soft, silky hand. "Do you need any dragons slain or hostile knights defeated? I'm your man."

She laughs again. Holy crap, I think I'm in love!

"Actually, I really need to see Chief Broebeck." She glances behind me toward the firehouse. "Is he here?"

"Uh...yeah. He's in his office....but he's married, you know. Whatever you need from him, I'll be happy to do for you."

She won't stop grinning at me. She takes my flirtations in stride... .and then, in front of my eyes, she pulls off her jacket.

I stare at her chest in stupid shock—and not because her round, full breasts show perfectly through her tight T-shirt.

She's wearing a Fire Department T-shirt—a Howe County Fire Department T-shirt.

"Chief Broebeck hired me to fill a position as a paramedic on your crew," she tells me. "I'm here for my first day of work. Could you please tell me where his office is?"

I have to summon every ounce of my willpower to tear my eyes away from her chest. I shut my mouth with an effort. "Um....I'm really sorry. Follow me. I'll take you to see him."

She only smiles at me. Her eyes glow with kindness and understanding. I'm going to have a hard time working with this woman. I can see that right now.

I turn around, leave the hose there, and lead Allison inside. She drapes her jacket over her arm so everyone can see her showing up in a Howe County Fire Department uniform.

We make it as far as the bottom of the stairs before Duke Broebeck comes down from his office.

"Duke!" I call out. "Allison Metcalfe is here for her first day of work."

I wave back and forth between them. Duke smiles at her and shakes her hand. "Great to see you. Come on in and I'll introduce you to everyone. This is Caleb Watts...."

Allison turns those heart-stopping eyes to me and smiles again. Is she blushing? "We met just now...outside."

"But not soon enough," I chime in. "Allison was just about to tell me about a big, fire-breathing dragon perched on the hill that she needs me to go slay for her."

She laughs again.

"Easy, big dog," Duke tells me. "It's her first day of work. Keep it clean."

"Slaying dragons is as clean as it gets. She wouldn't be there to clean up the blood. I would do that."

She laughs at that joke, too. Duke makes a face. "Go back to cleaning the driveway first, champ. Then we'll talk about dragon-slaying—but I don't think you're certified for that. You might need to take a few night courses."

Now it's my turn to laugh and Allison joins in. I start to walk away, but I'm all done hosing down the driveway.

I wind up the hose and go back inside to find the whole crew standing around talking to Allison. Duke is still there, too.

"John said you worked Back East for a while," Chris Daniels begins.

Allison's glowing expression fades. "Yeah, I'm really sorry to hear about what happened to Chief Brewer. He was such a great guy."

"We're making it through the day," Keith Brewer replies. "Are you from Howe? What made you move back to town?"

"She couldn't live without me," I tease. "Our destinies brought us back together."

Groans erupt around the circle and Billy Cates rolls his eyes to heaven. "Oh, here we go again. She walks into the firehouse, and five minutes later, you're love-bombing her to death."

"I'm just letting you all know in advance that we're made for each other." I look across the circle at Allison. "Just in case you didn't get the memo yet."

She laughs again. "Thank you for the warning." She turns to Duke. "So where am I rostered today?"

"I would normally put a new hire on one of the ambulances, but we've been so short-handed that I put you on the ladder truck today. Let me know if Caleb steps out of line." Duke points at me. "Do you hear that? I expect you to behave appropriately or you and I are going to have a discussion in my office. Understand?"

I raise both hands. "Since when have I ever acted like anything other than a perfect gentleman?"

"Perfect gentlemen don't start hitting on the new paramedic the minute she shows up for her first shift," Josh Abbott tells me. "Perfect gentlemen at least wait until the lunch break."

Everyone laughs and Carter Holt steps forward. "You're rostered with me on the ladder truck. Come with me and I'll show you around so you can orient to the truck."

Her features blanch when she sees the burn scars all over Carter's head, face, neck, and arms, but she recovers instantly and follows him.

I watch her walk away and admire the alternating contractions of her nice, juicy round ass under her uniform pants.

"Stop staring or the Chief will give you a smackdown," Josh murmurs in my ear.

"Mmm-mmm-mmm." I turn away shaking my head. "I'm in heaven."

I go back to helping Chris and Brooke Elsworth organize the linen closet. We fold up a bunch of towels, sheets, and blankets that have gotten messed up.

Then we unpack the new laundry, take it out of the bags from the delivery company, refold some of it, and stack it in the closet.

We're halfway through it when Carter and Allison come back. "Can I help?" Allison asks.

"You can help by giving me my heart back because I think you stole it," I tell her and make her blush again.

"We're gonna have to fit you with a shock collar." Carter pushes me to the other side of the circle and positions himself between me and Allison. "Put your tongue back in your mouth. You're drooling on the laundry."

Allison laughs. "It's nice to be appreciated. I'm flattered."

"Ouch!" I clutch at my heart. "There never was a crueler way to reject a guy than to tell him you're flattered."

"You better not let Duke hear you talking like that," Chris tells me. "You could get slapped with a sexual harassment complaint."

"Just for giving her a compliment? I don't think so."

I turn aside to put my latest folded towel on the shelf when the firehouse alarm goes off.

We drop what we're doing and head for our trucks.

I'm rostered on the rescue truck today, so I don't get to ride with Allison. I should probably be happy about that. I wouldn't want a woman that fine to distract me from my job.

"What's the call?!" Keith yells over to Billy when we pull out of the garage.

"Electrical accident at the power plant!" Billy calls back. "Unknown number of casualties—estimated at more than twenty!"

"Yikes!" Chris squeals behind me. "That's bad!"

We get to work pulling on our turnouts, but we don't put on our self-contained breathing apparatuses—not yet. We'll wait until we get to the scene to we see if we need them.

Duke's support pickup leads the way and the ladder truck and the two ambulances follow us out onto the highway. I completely forget about Allison. What will we find when we get to the scene?

Dozens of Police officers and power plant workers in high-vis clothing greet us at the entrance gate. They wave us to one side.

"We have thirty people over there," the plant manager tells us after we park and get out. "Some of them need medical attention and some of them don't. We have at least another twenty people trapped inside."

"Where are they?" Duke asks. "Is the power shut down to their location or are they still in danger?"

"We shut down power to the whole plant. We know where they are, but no one has dared to go back inside to get them. We didn't know if we should wait for you guys. We don't know how critical they are."

"Show us where they are." Duke turns around. "Josh and Chris—take Drew and George and start triage—but leave one ambulance here until we check the remaining patients. The rest of you come inside. If the patients aren't too critical, you can come back out and help with triage."

The crew splits up. The majority of us follow the plant manager inside the building.

Dozens of Police officers stand guard over the building. Other than that, the plant is deserted. Everyone else is already outside.

The plant manager stops at a heavily reinforced door. "The remaining patients are in here. This is where the short happened. They all got hit. We don't know how bad they are."

Duke nods. "Open it. We'll divide up—one paramedic and one firefighter to a patient unless we need to reassess." He goes through the group pairing us all off. "Caleb, you go with Carter. Danny, you go with Sophie. Keith—with Jessie. Billy—with Brooke. Ellis—with Allison. Vince—with Theo. Jacob—you're with me."

Chapter 2: Caleb

Carter gives me one quick nod before the plant manager opens the doors to let us inside the electrical plant.

We stream into a giant chamber full of electrical transformers. Our footsteps ring off the walls. The place sounds way too quiet.

The electrical workers lie all over the floor. Our teams split up. Carter and I head for the nearest worker.

We roll the guy over and instantly see that he's dead. Most of his face has been scorched off by electrical burns.

"He isn't breathing and he doesn't have a pulse." Carter connects the defibrillator to the guy's chest. The rest of his body is perfectly intact and untouched. "He doesn't have a rhythm. He's gone. Let's move on."

We head for one of the people the other teams aren't helping yet. Now that I get deeper into the room, I notice that not everyone in here is as unconscious as I thought they were.

Some of the workers move around on their own. The next guy we go to pushes himself up to sit on the floor. He cradles his head.

Carter kneels down next to him and starts checking the guy's pulse. "You okay, man?"

"I'm...yeah....." The guy looks around. "What happened?"

"The plant had a short. Look at me." Carter shines a light in the guy's eyes. "You have electrical burns on your hands. You probably got hit. Do you remember your name?"

"Mark....." the guy croaks. "Mark Flemming."

"Do you know what day it is?"

"Um.....it's Tuesday...."

"Do you think you can walk?" Carter asks.

"I....I think so....."

Carter and I help the guy stand up. He wobbles at first, but he walks just fine after that.

"Take him to the door and come straight back," Carter tells me. "Tell them to take him outside to the triage zone."

I escort Mark to the door. The plant workers take him off my hands.

I rejoin Carter in checking another dead body, but right then, we hear Allison yell from nearby. "We need some help over here!"

Carter and I race over to her and her patient. Ellis is already doing compressions on the guy.

"He doesn't have any superficial sign of injury," she tells us while she scrambles to start an IV. "His rhythm was thready and irregular before he crashed. Intubate him and check his pupils."

Carter tears open his jump kit and pulls out an ET tube and scope. I check the patient's pupils and start taking out the oxygen tank to set up Carter with a ventilator bag.

"His pupils are blown wide open!" I call over my shoulder. "One of his eyes is bloodshot."

"Set up the defibrillator, Caleb," she tells me. "Hurry."

I scramble to get out the defibrillator and attach the electrodes to the patient's chest. She's too busy shooting him full of drugs and Carter is just fitting the ET tube into place.

Ellis keeps doing compressions like a jackhammer through the whole call.

Sweat drips from his hair and falls on the patient's chest when I attach the electrodes. I glance up at Ellis. "You okay to keep going for now?"

He nods without making eye contact.

"Tell me if you get tired. We can swap."

He nods again and we both get back to work. I switch on the defibrillator.

Just then, we hear a choking noise from one of the other nearby patients. "Bag him, Caleb," Carter orders and passes me the bag so he can scoot over and check the other patient.

I pump the bag with one hand and start the defibrillator cycle with the other. "Stand clear!"

Ellis and Allison back off instantly. The patient is in V-tach. Ellis goes back to doing compressions.

Allison finishes injecting the patient with a bunch of drugs. "We need to transport. Caleb, go back to the ambulance and bring in a gurney."

I nod, but before I can stand up, Ellis makes a little gasping noise in his throat. He's too dedicated to say he wants to stop doing compressions, but just then, the defibrillator indicates another assessment cycle.

"Stand clear!" I call out. Ellis moves back. "You go get the gurney. I'll take over compressions."

He nods and leaves. As soon as the defibrillator reads another v-tach cycle, I start compressions.

Allison bags the patient with one hand and does a million other things with her other hand. She glances up at me. "Thanks for your help."

I look past her toward Carter. He's helping another patient sit up. "I guess he doesn't need me now."

Allison's eyes dart sideways. "Why is Ellis so quiet? He wouldn't look at me or talk to me at all—but he did everything I told him to. He jumped right in when I told him to do compressions."

"He's a good guy. He's a very dedicated firefighter. You won't have any problem with him."

"What's wrong with him? Is he mute or something?"

"No, not at all. He was a jokester before this happened."

"Before what happened?"

I lower my voice so only she can hear me. "The guy who shot John Brewer....he was trying to shoot Carter. Ellis tackled Carter out of the way and saved his life. The shot hit John instead. Ellis blames himself for John's death. Ellis hardly talks at all now. He doesn't socialize with us or even look at us. He keeps to himself as much as possible." I shake my head. "It's a shame because he's such an awesome guy."

We have to stop talking when Ellis comes back with the gurney.

Carter finishes with his patient at the same time and comes back to help us load our patient. I have to keep doing compressions, and on the third defibrillation cycle, the guy snaps back into a sinus rhythm.

"Yes!" Allison cheers. "Wonderful. Load him up. Take his blood pressure, Caleb."

I walk along next to the gurney on the way outside. "His pressure is three hundred over one hundred and fifty."

"His brain must have gotten fried," she mumbles.

"What do you want me to do?" I ask.

"You can go back to working with Carter the way Chief Broebeck said. You come with me, Ellis. I need you to ride back to the hospital with me in case the guy codes and we need to start compressions again."

Ellis nods and walks out of the plant with her. Carter and I go back inside. I spend the rest of the call helping the other firefighters and paramedics with their patients.

I pass Allison a few times both at the scene and the hospital, but I don't get a chance to talk to her.

Talking to her, flirting with her, and spending time with her are the last things on my mind right now.

We make it back to the firehouse just ten minutes before the shift changes. The second crew is already there waiting to take over for us.

We spend the last few minutes restocking the trucks. I get to the supply closet to get some bandages and find Allison in there alone.

"Way to save the day, Lady Badass," I tell her. "You can give me mouth-to-mouth anytime."

She blushes and grins at me. "It sounds to me like you're respirating just fine."

She pushes past me to leave the closet. I should finish my job, but the temptation to talk to her proves irresistible.

I follow her back out to the garage. "Do you want to go out sometime? There's a really cool fun park across town. They have go-karts, minigolf, a video arcade, bowling alley—everything. What do you say?"

She turns around to face me, but right then, Duke walks out from behind the rescue truck in time to hear me ask her out.

"Back off, Romeo," he tells me. "You made your feelings clear. If she wants to go out with you, she'll let you know."

I glance at Allison. She doesn't leap in to say that she will go out with me.

Her eyes glow with understanding and warmth—almost affection—but she still doesn't answer.

She answers by not answering. She couldn't make it clearer if she flashed me a neon sign.

My shoulders slump and I turn away. I mumble, "Yes, Sir," and go back to work.

Chapter 3: Allison

The fire alarm goes off in the firehouse and everyone in the staff breakroom stops what they're doing. We all pour down the stairs and load into the vehicles.

I'm rostered on the rescue truck with Carter Holt as the other paramedic. I'm getting used to his shocking appearance after a week of working on this crew.

No one else on the crew seems to notice the way he looks and I'm starting to understand why. He's such a great guy and he's an exceptional paramedic.

After a while, I only notice his personality. What he looks like doesn't seem to matter anymore.

Danny Brewer, Caleb Watts, and Ellis Barrett sit in the middle seat with Keith Brewer and Billy Cates upfront.

They've all been over-the-top nice to me and welcomed me to the crew. I couldn't ask for a more welcoming reception.

This crew is really amazing. They're all so close and supportive of each other. I haven't been able to pick up any underlying hostilities, cliquish behavior, or toxic attitudes from anyone.

I can't say Ellis has been nice and welcoming, but he sure is helpful. He never hesitates to help me and the others whenever he sees a need.

It's eerie how quiet he is, especially when I keep hearing from everyone how outgoing and funny he used to be.

Chief Brewer's death must have hit him really hard, but the rest of the crew seems to take that in stride, too. They don't push Ellis out. They just accept that this is the way he is now.

I don't see anyone trying to talk him out of it or change his behavior—or maybe they already tried and gave up.

The others treat him just as warmly. Danny, Caleb, and Ellis check their equipment on the way to the call.

"We got a fire alarm going off in an office building downtown!" Billy reads on the computer. "The employees are all still evacuating, so no one knows if anyone is still inside."

Caleb points at something on Ellis's SCBA. "Tighten the hose nozzle. It's coming loose."

I barely look up from the jump kit Carter and I are zipping closed. I only look to see what Caleb and Ellis are talking about.

"The O-ring is broken," I tell them. "That mask is no good for this call. Here. Use mine."

I put the jump kit aside, detach the mask from my SCBA, and hand it to them over the back of their seat. Caleb takes the mask. "Thank you."

I smile at him. "Pull the O-ring so no one makes a mistake and tries to use the apparatus on this call. Leave the hose detached and disconnect the mask from the apparatus to make it obvious that the unit is unusable."

Caleb and Ellis exchange glances. "Duke won't like this," Caleb replies.

"I'll explain it to him. I'll get him to assign me to triage outside the building for this call. I won't need an SCBA." I glance at Ellis. "You better attach it before we get there."

He gets to work. Caleb thanks me again over the back of the seat.

I catch him making eye contact with me, but only for a split second before he turns around and goes back to helping Ellis with the apparatus.

Caleb has been exceptionally polite to me ever since Chief Broebeck told him to back off from flirting with me. Caleb hasn't said a single word to me that was anything less than perfectly professional.

I do notice him making significant eye contact with me at times—and watching me when he thinks I don't notice. He hasn't lost interest.

I have heard through the firehouse grapevine that he's been hounding Chief Broebeck for permission to ask me out again.

I can't say Caleb isn't attractive. He definitely is and he has a wonderful, fun-loving, easy-going personality.

He isn't the biggest firefighter on the crew. He isn't as big as Keith or Billy, but Caleb is just as muscular in a leaner, athletic way. He's only a few inches taller than I am, but that somehow makes him seem more accessible and less intimidating than the others.

I can't help but feel drawn to his soft brown hair and boyish features. His deep brown eyes sparkle with fun mixed with plenty of compassion and caring.

He's highly professional during calls and dedicated to his crew and the job. I've never seen him slacking off or doing anything out of line—ever.

He doesn't turn around to look at me again. No one would ever guess he could act so flirtatious. He pretends that he never asked me out—or that he said anything about me giving him mouth-to-mouth—or that he ever suggested I stole his heart.

We get to the scene and Chief Broebeck meets the rescue truck to assign us all to our jobs. I have to interrupt him to tell him about Ellis's SCBA and to request that the Chief assign me to triage instead.

He agrees and I join up with Chris and the EMTs. We start going through the employees who are already standing outside the building.

We run into one of the managers who is going through the crowd. She marks off the names of everyone present to take a head count on the employees.

We don't find any injuries. Everyone is okay. They're just anxious.

We come to the end of the crowd and check in with the manager. "Everyone is accounted for," she tells me. "There should be no one left in the building."

I go over to Chief Broebeck to tell him the news and that none of the evacuees needs any medical treatment.

He gets on the radio. "Are you finding anything?"

Keith answers him. "There's nothing in here—no fire—no casualties—nothing. It's all clear."

"Come on out and let's go home." Chief Broebeck turns to me and Chris. "You two can pack up."

We have nothing to pack up. We put away our jump kits and drug boxes. Then we just have to stand around and wait for the fire crew to come out of the building.

The crew loads up and heads back to the firehouse while the building employees go inside and return to work. We don't even need to restock our trucks since we didn't do anything.

Ellis hands me my SCBA mask on the way there. "Thank you again," Caleb tells me. "You're a lifesaver."

"Do you have the replacement O-rings at the firehouse?" I ask. "You can replace it in a few seconds."

"I don't think so. Duke will probably want to send the whole apparatus in for a maintenance check."

I frown at him. "Isn't that overkill? Just replace the ring and you're good to go. We always did it that way at my other jobs."

"You tell him that," Caleb remarks over his shoulder. "He has his own way of doing things."

I hesitate and then thrust my hand across the seat. "Give me the mask. I'll deal with it."

Caleb shakes his head when he hands it over. "It's your funeral. Duke doesn't like people questioning his decisions."

"I'm not questioning his decision because I don't even know what his decision is. I'll talk to him about it and find out what he wants to do. It's silly that we would be down an entire apparatus over a fifty-cent O-ring we could replace in a matter of minutes."

"Just don't tell him it's silly," Caleb returns. "He could take it the wrong way."

I frown at the side of his head. "He seems more reasonable than that. Surely you can explain these things to him and get him to understand the logic of doing it this way."

"Maybe you or one of the other paramedics could."

"Why not you? You're a member of this crew in good standing. It isn't like you're on disciplinary probation for insubordination or bad attitude. Why wouldn't he listen to you?"

"I don't know if he would. I wouldn't want him to put me on probation for anything."

"So you wouldn't even ask him?" I counter. "I can't believe I'm hearing this. I thought you liked him."

"I do like him. I'm saying I would ask him instead of telling him it's silly to do it a different way than he decided. I might suggest it.

I wouldn't outright tell him it was silly to do it another way. He wouldn't appreciate that."

I blink at him. He looks back at me with his deep steady gaze. "Oh," I mumble. "I see what you mean."

He turns around and goes back to arranging his turnouts under the seat. I become aware of Ellis and Carter both listening to our conversation.

Carter doesn't get involved and Ellis never says anything anyway.

I can't deny that he's listening, though. His features register more interest in our conversation than I've seen from him before—or maybe I'm just noticing it more now.

Maybe he's always been interested from a distance and I just haven't gotten to know these people well enough yet.

Chapter 4: Allison

The crew returns to the firehouse. I take Ellis's SCBA mask over to Duke and show him the broken O-ring.

"Caleb says you would want to send the mask in for maintenance," I tell him. "We always just replaced the rings and kept going at my former jobs."

He barely looks at the mask. He keeps working on one of the oxygen tank regulators. He doesn't stop while he talks to me. "No, we'll send it in. The ring wouldn't get broken down unless there was something wrong with the seal between the hose and the connector. The firefighters who are using this apparatus probably keep tightening it and tightening it and tightening it just to get a decent seal. We need to check to make sure there's nothing wrong with the connector. Besides, we can't take any chances after our recent problems. We'll err on the side of caution and send it in."

I would probably have argued back at him if this was any other firehouse.

My conversation with Caleb comes back to me. Duke Broebeck is Fire Chief of this crew. His decision is final. It would only annoy him if a new hire questioned his decisions.

He notices my hesitation. "Is something wrong?"

I clear my throat. "Would you mind.....just to satisfy my curiosity ....would you mind telling me what recent problems would make you do this? I know it isn't my business. I'm just curious."

He stops what he's doing, straightens up, and faces me. "The man who shot John Brewer tried to kill Carter once before the fatal shooting. The guy sabotaged Carter's SCBA by tampering with the seals between the hoses and the mask—the same seals this O-ring is supposed to protect. Everyone on the crew is extremely sensitive about their SCBAs now. You need to know that going forward. It could explain why the crew keeps tightening the connector too much—or it could be the other way around. They might have to tighten it so much because there's something wrong with it. We need to check to find out which one it is."

I gulp. "Oh. I didn't know."

"That's why I'm telling you." He waves the mask at me. "Thank you for bringing it to my attention. I'm sure Ellis is grateful—as are we all."

"I.....I'm sorry I brought it up. I'll be more understanding about it in the future."

"No problem." He bends back over his work. "No one expects you to know everything right from the jump."

I make a tactful retreat and send up a silent prayer of thanks to Caleb for talking some sense into me before I confronted the Chief about this.

Of course a guy as level-headed as Duke Broebeck would have his reasons to make that decision—and every other decision. Of course he would consider it out of line if I challenged those decisions.

I really need to pull my head in around here. I might be an experienced paramedic, but I don't run this operation. He does.

I finish the shift, get my stuff out of my locker, and head out to the parking lot to leave for the day.

I'm just about to get into my car when Caleb comes out of the firehouse behind me.

He bursts into one of his old grins. "Hey! Maid Marian!"

I laugh at him. "Who are you—Friar Tuck?"

He winces in mock pain and grabs his stomach. "I'm going to have to go on a diet now."

I let myself cast one glance at his washboard abs before I turn back to my car. "I think you're just fine, champ."

"Allison—wait!" He takes a step forward and stops himself. "Thank you—for telling us about Ellis's mask."

"You said that already. I'm here to help the crew in any way I can."

"Hey! Do you want to go out sometime? You never answered me before Duke stepped in. What do you say? We both have tomorrow off. We could go out in the evening. I could pick you up."

I turn around and find myself smiling at him. "I'm really flattered, Caleb. You've been nothing but sweet to me since I started here and I'm really grateful—but I'm already with someone. I'm engaged."

His features drain of all color. "Oh. I'm so sorry. I had no idea. I wouldn't have asked you out if I knew."

"I know! I should have told you before, but I didn't want to knock you down in front of the whole crew. I think you're a really special guy, very attractive and very nice. If I was single, I would love to go out with you, but I've been in a relationship with my fiancé for over two years. We've been long-distance until now and I moved here to be with him. We both moved halfway to meet in the middle. See? I'm sorry. I really don't mean to hurt your feelings. Maybe that's another reason I didn't tell you. You're a really nice guy....."

He makes a face. "Please. You did not just call me a nice guy."

I find myself laughing. "I didn't mean it like that. I would jump at the chance to go out with you if I wasn't already with someone."

He frowns for a second and then brightens up almost instant-ly. "Okay, well, we're having a firehouse barbecue on Saturday. You should come. I mean—the whole crew is. One of them probably already invited you...."

"No, they haven't. This is the first I've heard about it."

His eyes pop and his jaw drops. "No one has invited you?! Really?"

"Nope. I didn't know anything about it."

"Okay, well, then, let me be the first. You should come. I'm not asking you out or anything. Everyone at the firehouse goes—and plenty of people bring their non-firehouse spouses and partners. You should bring your fiancé so we can all get to know him. Who is he?"

"He's a doctor at the hospital. He just started there when we moved here together."

He frowns and rubs his chin. "Hmm. Maybe Ellen knows him."

"Who's Ellen?"

"John Brewer's widow. She used to be a paramedic here, but she suffered an injury that left her disabled and she had to quit. She's works as a paramedic in the ED now."

My eyes fly open. "Oh, her! The lady with the dark hair and the leg brace."

"Yes!" He points at me and smiles. "That's her. She and Leila Cun-ningham—that's Keith's wife—she's on maternity leave now—they usually organize the barbecues. That may be why no one has invited you—but that doesn't matter. You should bring your fiancé along. Then we can all give him a hard time the same way we give everyone a hard time."

I laugh in pure relief. "Thanks for not taking it personally."

"No way! You should have told me right off the bat. Then I wouldn't have been making a dope out of myself by hitting on you. I'm really sorry about that."

"Don't worry about it. It was really sweet and you're super funny. It's nice to be appreciated."

"Well.....you're such a great member of our crew. We're all happy you're here. You don't know the nightmare we've had trying to find people who fit in with us. We couldn't be happier." He raises his hands. "I swear you won't have any more problems with me. Scout's honor."

I beam at him. "Thank you. I really enjoy working with you, too."

He smiles back and jerks his thumb over his shoulder. "I better go. Have a good one. I'll see you at the barbecue."

I wave at him and we both back away toward our vehicles. He gets into a shiny blue pickup with a camper shell on the back and a rack on top.

He waves again when he pulls out of the parking lot and drives away down the street. Now my secret is out.

It's only a matter of time before the rest of the fire crew finds out that I have a fiancé and that I moved to Howe so we could be together.

Chapter 5: Caleb

I get out of my pickup and squint down the beach. I'm the first person here.

I lift the barbecue out of the truck bed, carry it down to the picnic table, and jam the legs of the barbecue into the sand at a distance from where everyone usually stands around talking.

I go back and forth to my truck, dump a bunch of charcoal into the barbecue, douse it with lighter fluid, and set it alight so it will burn down by the time the Brewers show up to start grilling.

I'm just going back for my coolers of burgers, steaks, sausages, and other grillables when Keith shows up with Leila and baby Leon. Ellen rolls in a minute later with Oakleigh in the back seat.

Oakleigh gets out and walks off by herself into the dunes while the rest of us are still hugging and saying hello.

"No improvement in the munchkin?" I ask Ellen.

She shakes her head and grimaces. "No change."

"She's all right," Keith interjects. "We can't blame her for being sad."

"I don't blame her for being sad," Ellen replies. "I'm sad. We're all sad. We're just adults and we know how to handle things better than she does. Come on. Let's go put on some pounds."

We talk and joke on our way down to the barbecue. The fire trucks and ambulances show up later and the crew floods the beach along with the other off-duty crew members.

Conversation, drinks, and banter are already flowing when Allison shows up with the guy I assume is her fiancé. He's a tall guy with a runner's build and curly reddish-brown hair.

He has a bookish appearance. He really does look like a doctor. She introduces him all around. "This is my fiancé, Clay Wescott. Some of you may have already met him in the ED."

I haven't met him in the ED, but the others obviously have. He and Ellen actually hug each other like they're the best of friends.

He shakes my hand the same as everyone else when Allison introduces us. Then he joins the circle while we all talk.

"Did you hear about the girl we transported yesterday who got a marble stuck up her nostril?" I ask.

Allison howls, throws up her hands, and turns away laughing. "Do you have to bring that up?! We're about to start eating in a minute."

"I helped treat her," Ellen chimes in. "They had to make an incision in her nostril. The skin was stretched too tightly to get the marble out any other way."

"You should have seen it," I tell the others. "Her nostril looked like a balloon."

"How did she get it in there?" Sophie asks. "That's what I can't understand."

"I don't understand what would make a person want to stick a marble in their nostril in the first place," Danny adds. "I mean, walk me through the thought process here. There you are, playing with your marbles, and you think to yourself, 'Here's a nice green one. I need a nice safe place to keep it where it won't get lost. Where can I stash it so no one will ever find it?'"

We all laugh. "Was she in distress?" Leila asks. "Was she in a lot of pain?"

"I don't think she even realized it was up there." Allison turns to me. "Did you notice her in distress? She seemed confused about why we were making such a fuss over her."

"Do you remember the way she was talking?" I ask. "She sounded like she had a really bad case of nasal congestion."

She laughs again. "She did have a really bad case of nasal congestion."

"She kept trying to pick her nose and shoving it farther up there," I go on. "The doctors at the ED were worried it would actually go up into her sinuses. They wouldn't have been able to get it out at all. That's why they used an incision."

"Imagine trying to explain the scar to your future boyfriends," Allison suggests. "'So, sweetie, how did you get that scar on your nose? I'm just curious.'"

We all laugh again, including me, but just then, Duke shows up with his wife Naomi and their little baby daughter Amelia.

Duke twists the cap off his beer bottle and joins our group while Naomi sits down at the picnic table next to Leila. "What are we talking about?" Duke asks.

"Don't ask," Ellen asks.

"I just did," he replies.

"You need to have a conversation with Amelia when she gets old enough to start kindergarten," Danny tells him. "Explain to her not to put any object in her nostrils or her ears."

"Or any other orifice," I add and the whole circle explodes.

"You might want to have that conversation with her again when she gets to high school," Jessie teases.

Duke turns bright red. "Amelia won't be going to high school because she is never going to get that old. I can't handle it."

We laugh at him and Keith claps him on the shoulder. "You need a crash helmet, man."

"You're gonna be great," Carter tells him. "She'll be fine. She'll be better than fine. She'll be stunning."

"That's what I'm worried about," Duke mutters.

Sophie turns to Clay. He's been quiet since he got here, but then again, he isn't in on the whole fire crew joke.

"Which department are you in at the hospital?" she asks. "We haven't seen you in the ED yet."

"I'm in orthopedics," he replies. "I've gotten called down to the ED a few times, but I don't get called in unless a patient has a broken bone the ED staff can't handle—or it goes to surgery."

"That's cool!" Jessie replies. "Where were you before this?"

"Whitley," he replies. "I went to medical school there, did my residency there, and then got a job there afterward. I've been there the whole time."

"I worked in Whitley," Carter chimes in. "I think I remember you."

Clay looks away. "I definitely remember you."

"You would have to be blind not to," Danny remarks.

"So how did you two meet?" I ask. "Allison said you were long-distance before you moved to Howe."

Clay glances at me and then pretends to wipe the dew off his beer bottle. "We met at a house concert in Woodhurst. My sister's family lives there. I went down there to visit them and I went to the concert while I was in town."

"I lived in Woodhurst before this," Allison adds. "That's where we met....and the rest is history."

"Oh, yeah, John mentioned that you worked in Woodhurst before," I reply. "The town awash in O-rings."

She laughs. Only a few other people from the rescue truck join in. Ellis stands off to one side, so he isn't close enough to hear the reference.

He's rostered on duty today, so he has to come to the barbecue. He wouldn't come if he wasn't on duty.

The conversation breaks up into a few different clusters. I go over to the grill to help Keith, but he's so territorial about the barbecue that I wind up backing off.

I return to the picnic table to get myself something to eat when Duke comes over to me. "Could you help me, man?" he asks. "Naomi made a bunch of food, but she has her hands full. Help me unload my truck."

"Okay. No problem." I follow him to the parking lot.

Naomi made more than a bunch of food. We unload multiple boxes of homemade cookies, desserts, and a truckload of sandwiches and other munchies.

We take everything back down to the picnic table. The two mothers aren't there anymore. Naomi paces up and down the sand holding Amelia and singing to her.

Leila kneels in the sand at a distance from the group. She's laid out a blanket on the sand where she can change Leon's diaper without disturbing anyone.

I have to rearrange the stuff on the picnic table to make room for everything and we haven't even finished unloading Duke's truck.

I'm just about to leave when I spot Clay and Allison walking away down the beach. They walk side by side without looking back at anyone. That lucky bastard. Does he even know what a prize he got when he met her?

I'm not thinking about that because she's as taken as she can possibly be. I go back to Duke's truck to get the next load. He comes with me, but just as he's turning away from the picnic table, Naomi comes toward him to ask him something.

I go back to the parking lot by myself, stack up the three remaining boxes, and take them back down to the barbecue.

By the time I get there, Duke is holding Amelia while Naomi rummages in her enormous bag of stuffed supplies.

I don't want to get involved in whatever emergency they're dealing with, so I deal with the food situation on my own.

The table is already groaning with more food than the crew can safely eat in a year, so I stack the boxes out of the way on the ground.

I straighten up to finally get my own lunch when I see Clay and Allison standing face to face down the beach. They're far enough away that I can't hear either of their voices. I can see enough just from their body language.

They hold an intense conversation with both of them gesticulating and chopping the air. Each of them points in a different direction, shakes their heads, and waves at each other. That doesn't look good, but I'm not getting involved in that, either.

I turn away and concentrate on my food. I pretend not to see them, take my plate back to the group, and wedge myself in. I keep my back to the couple while they argue.

Whatever happens in their relationship doesn't concern me. Allison is my co-worker—nothing more. I put it completely out of my mind that I was ever interested in her.

Chapter 6: Allison

I slam my locker shut and head out to the garage to start my shift. I find Chris already in the back of the rescue truck going through the drug box.

"Hey!" I call up to her. "I'm with you today."

She grins at me. "Come on up. You can do the jump kit while I do this."

I get into the seat next to her and unzip the jump kit. Caleb sits in the seat in front of me talking to Billy, who is in the front seat checking the radios and computer transmission signals.

Neither of them turns around when Chris and I start discussing the items in both the drug box and the jump kit.

"It looks like we're low on moldable splints," I tell her. "I'm going to get some more."

No one notices when I leave and come back. We spend another five minutes going over everything before the fire alarm goes off.

Billy and Caleb look around. They, Chris, and I are already in the truck. We don't have to go anywhere.

Keith, Ellis, and Danny show up a minute later and climb in with us. Keith starts the motor and we pull out onto the road.

"Motor vehicle accident!" Billy tells us. "One patient—lost control of his car and drove through the K-rail."

"He drove *through* the K-rail?" Caleb asks. "The K-rail is a concrete barricade. He would have had to jump the K-rail and go over it."

"I'm just reading what's in the notes, pal!" Billy calls over his shoulder. "Take it up with dispatch. Police are on scene. They say the car is down an embankment and needs extrication."

"Swell," Keith growls.

Chris smirks at me. "Aren't you glad you got the extra splints now?"

We don't have a chance to talk anymore before we get out onto the highway. The whole four-lane highway is completely jammed with wall-to-wall traffic.

Police officers direct Keith to drive down the shoulder to the scene. The Police have cordoned off two lanes for us to work while the traffic inches through the bottleneck in the other two lanes.

We get out of the truck and peer down the embankment. The car in question lies half buried in bushes. We can't even see the patient from here.

Duke gets out of his support truck and starts giving orders.

"Medical personnel stand back out of the way. Fire crew—back the rescue truck up to the shoulder, set up your outriggers, and attach your winch to the rear axle to pull out the car."

"What about the patient?" Sophie asks.

"The embankment is too steep," Duke replies. "We'll bring the car up to level ground, block it off, and then extricate. Let's go!"

The fire crew gets to work. Chris, Sophie, Jessie, and I stand off to one side with the two EMTs from the ambulances.

We just have to wait while the guys winch the car up the embankment. As soon as they pull it out of the bushes, we can all see that there's only one patient inside—the driver of the car.

"Jessie and George, you can take the ambulance back to the fire-house," Duke orders. "We won't need more than one ambulance and we have enough paramedics on scene already."

They leave, and in a little while, he sends the ladder truck away, too. That leaves the rescue truck and one ambulance.

The guys pull the car into the two roped-off lanes, block the vehicle, and start carving into the driver's compartment.

The driver lies unconscious in the seat with blood all over his face and chest. We can't see anything else about his condition until the guys use the Jaws of Life to carve open the ruined car.

Chris and I rush in to assess his injuries. Chris climbs into the car through the passenger side while I do my best to take the patient's vitals from outside where the driver's door used to be.

"He has a hemothorax with a flail chest and bloody sputum coming out of his mouth!" I tell her. Then I yell over my shoulder. "We need a backboard, full C-spine restraints, and a gurney over here on the double!"

Caleb appears out of nowhere with a backboard. No way could he have gone back to the ambulance to get the board. He must have already been bringing it over before I said anything.

Ellis doesn't wait to be told before he slots into the back seat and takes hold of the patient's head. Ellis holds the patient's spine immobile while I swivel out of the way.

I call instructions to Ellis and Caleb to tilt the patient sideways so Caleb can slide the backboard under the patient's hips.

Billy hands me a cervical collar. I have to go through a detailed negotiation with Ellis to get the collar on the patient. Ellis does everything perfectly. He's obviously attended a lot of these calls and knows exactly what to do.

Caleb has to wedge himself right up against my body to get hold of the patient so we can lie him down on the backboard. Ellis hands off the patient's head to me and Chris gets ready to take the head from me as soon as we tilt the patient sideways.

"His pelvis is shattered!" Caleb tells me. "There's nothing to him. It looks like both legs are broken, too."

"Take hold of his pants so you don't put pressure on his fractures," I tell him. "Get ready—on three. One—two—three!"

We swivel and rotate the patient sideways to lie him down. As soon as we start moving him, I realize Caleb is right.

The airbag didn't deploy, so the guy must have hit the steering wheel and dashboard full force. He broke nearly every bone in his body.

Chris and I have to work fast to stabilize him. Caleb, Ellis, and Billy revolve around us working just as fast to restrain the patient to the board so we can transport.

The five of us keep bumping into each other, sticking our arms in each other's faces, and calling instructions and orders back and forth to each other.

"We're ready!" Caleb tells us. "He's ready to move!"

"Go!" I tell him.

The guys pull the patient onto the waiting gurney. Chris and I crowd around him working our fastest to stabilize him, but almost as soon as we leave the car, he codes.

"He's crashing!" I yell. "Start compressions!"

Caleb steps onto the gurney's lower bar and starts doing compressions. "There's nothing to him!" he calls out. "His sternum is offering no resistance at all!"

None of us has time to mess with that. Chris intubates the patient while I get busy shooting drugs into his IV.

Billy, Ellis, and the others wheel us to the waiting ambulance, shut us in, and Drew drives us off into town.

Chris and I have to work around Caleb to listen to the patient's lung sounds and keep taking his vitals. I accidentally bump into Caleb when I move up to the patient's head to test his pupils.

"Both pupils blown out! He probably has multiple head injuries, too."

"What the hell *isn't* wrong with this guy?" Caleb mutters.

"Stand clear!" I call out as the defibrillator goes off.

Caleb collapses back on the bench seat, passes his sweaty forehead across his shoulder, and immediately gets back onto the gurney to start compressions again as soon as I tell him to.

All three of us are still going full steam when Drew opens the doors and the medical team surrounds us. Caleb doesn't stop doing compressions even for a minute.

I get all mixed up with the medical team and help them move the patient to the hospital gurney. They make only the barest check on the patient's status and take Chris's report before another defibrillation cycle comes around.

"Stand clear!" one of the doctors calls.

Caleb steps away, and when the defibrillator reads that he's still in v-fib, one of the hospital medics takes over doing compressions.

Caleb and I stand back and watch the medical team wheel the patient out of sight. I turn to Caleb. "Are you all right?"

"Yeah!" he pants and lifts his shirt up to wipe the sweat off his face.

He doesn't realize when he does it that he exposes his midsection. I catch a glimpse of his rock-hard stomach, but that's nothing I didn't already know about. I can see his physique through his uniform.

He turns away still breathing heavily. "I'm gonna go hose myself down. I'll be back."

I squeeze his shoulder. "You did great. Thank you so much."

He smiles at me and walks away. I go to the hospital supply room and start gathering up replacement supplies of all the drugs and equipment we used on that patient.

I'm just picking up everything to take it back to the ambulance when Clay walks into the supply room.

"Hey, sweetie!" I exclaim. "How's your day going?"

He takes a step closer to me and bends down to get right in my face. "Don't you sweetie me! I got called down to the ED for an orthopedic consult on that patient with the shattered pelvis. I saw you practically with your arms around Caleb Watts just now."

I spin around to stare at him, but I have to immediately pull back when I realize how closely he's crowding me into the corner. "I don't know what you're talking about!" I counter. "Caleb and I were taking care of the patient! You saw that. Caleb was doing compressions and I was....."

"Don't you dare lie to me!" he hisses. "I saw you with my own eyes! You were practically lying right on top of him!"

I open my mouth to argue back, but I stop myself. I realize in that moment that I'm backed up all the way against the supply room wall. Clay blocks the only way out of here.

He glares in my face with such fury that I actually start to get worried. Is he about to get violent with me?

"I already told you to keep away from him!" Clay snarls. "It's bad enough that you were flirting with him right in front of me and all the rest of your crew at the barbecue...."

"I wasn't flirting with him! I was talking to him exactly the same way everyone else at the barbecue was talking to him."

"You lying bitch!" he snaps way too loudly. "I'm not blind! You have a thing for him ever since he asked you out."

"I told you he asked me out! I told you so you would understand that I handled it. I told you so you would understand that I never gave him any reason to think anything could happen between us. I told you to put your mind at rest, not so you could go off on me and accuse us of something that isn't happening."

He raises his eyebrows in the worst possible way. "*Us?* You're calling you and Caleb '*us*'?"

"No, Clay! When are you going to let this go? There's nothing going on between me and Caleb. I told him I was with you and he dropped it completely. He respects our relationship. What happened between us is just professional interaction! You know that!"

"What I saw was NOT professional interaction," he snarls. "I don't want you working with him anymore. You'll just have to tell Chief Broebeck to roster you on opposite shifts as Caleb so you don't work together anymore."

My jaw drops. "You can't be serious! That might not even be possible! The firehouse is already shorthanded enough."

He clenches his teeth in brutal fury and snarls under his breath. I've never seen or heard him like this. "If you don't—if you ever work on another shift with Caleb again—we're done. Understand? It's over between us. You go talk to Chief Broebeck and get your schedule changed. If you don't, I'll know you care more about Caleb Watts than you do about me."

He storms out of the supply room and leaves me standing there dumbfounded. This can't be happening.

Everything was going perfectly between me and Clay before we moved to Howe to live together. What was I supposed to do—lie to him by not telling him that Caleb asked me out?

I thought he would be relieved that I was being honest with him.

Now he's carrying some kind of vendetta against Caleb.

I go over every detail of that call in my mind. Yes, I bumped into Caleb more times than I can count. I even had to lean against him when we were extricating the patient.

Touching him like that and working so closely with him didn't mean anything to me. I'm certain it didn't mean anything to him, either.

I would have done exactly the same thing with a female paramedic or with any of the married firefighters. None of us thought anything about it. We were too preoccupied with taking care of the patient.

I can't tell Chief Broebeck about this. I don't dare to.

I've been working at Howe Firehouse for less than two weeks. I can't start bringing him personnel problems so soon. I can't start causing problems for my co-workers, either. They're just trying to do their jobs.

I can't find any fault in Caleb's behavior on that call. Everything he did was perfectly professional. He would never jeopardize a patient or crew cohesion by bringing anything personal into a call.

He wouldn't jeopardize crew cohesion by hitting on me after I told him I was with someone else. That's the kind of guy he is. He just dropped the whole thing. That on its own tells me all I need to know about him.

I can't think about that right now. I have a job to do.

I shake those thoughts out of my head. I'll think about it another time and decide how I want to deal with Clay, Caleb, and Chief Broebeck.

I take my supplies back to the ambulance. I'm just putting everything away for the trip back when Caleb shows up with his hair wet.

He gets into the front seat with Drew while Chris and I ride in the back on our way to the firehouse.

Chapter 7: Caleb

I bend over the pool table, strike my cue into the cue ball, and send it rolling down the table. The cue ball hits the solid red ball, bounces off at an angle, and the cue ball and the red ball hit other balls to sink them both.

"Nice one, Ace," my brother Amos tells me. "Have you been practicing behind my back?"

"Maybe I'm just bored and I have nothing else to do." I sink three more balls before I miss.

I go back to the counter to take a swig of my drink while he approaches the table.

"I'm playing the winner," my friend Buck calls from a nearby stool.

"You only said that twelve times in the last ten minutes," Amos calls over his shoulder and misses his first stroke. "You'll be playing Caleb at the rate we're going."

"Don't feel too bad, big brother," I tell him. "Maybe, one day, with a lot of development, you just might attain my level of awesomeness."

He snorts and picks up his beer bottle. "That shouldn't be too hard."

I bend over to take my next shot, but I pause when I hear a commotion at the bar across the room.

I glance up and freeze when I see Allison sitting on a bar stool. She's wearing an absolutely jaw-dropping red minidress, lipstick-red pumps, and an extra-small, tight white cropped jacket over her arms and shoulders.

The dress and her position on the bar stool give me a mouth-watering view of the voluptuous curve of her waist, hips, ass, and thighs. I'm looking at her from directly behind. God damn, she is so fine!

Her wavy blonde hair cascades over her shoulders in a golden torrent. It's a good thing I can't see her face from here or I might just melt into a puddle of goo on the floor.

She's all by herself sitting on a bar stool. I glance around for Clay, but I don't see him, so maybe she's here with friends.

She's dressed up too much for that—and she's dressed up too much to be here alone—not when she has a fiancé at home.

"Don't get distracted and miss your aim," Amos teases me from behind. "You might have to go home and take a cold shower."

I tear my eyes away from the view to make my shot, but he's right. Seeing Allison like that does distract me. I miss and retreat to the counter to nurse my beer in peace.

This gives me another chance to gaze at her across the bar. The game is the last thing on my mind.

I'm just settling in to watch her from afar when another guy shoulders up to the bar next to her. He leans in way too close, tries to talk to her, and loses his balance. He's drunk off his ass and almost falls on top of her.

She rears back and tries to push him away, but he's way too big. He dives in and tries to kiss her, but she dodges.

I cross the bar in a heartbeat and push the guy off. "Hey, pal," I tell him. "Leave the lady alone."

He can barely see straight enough to focus on me. He looks off to one side when he tries to confront me.

I shove my arm between him and Allison and then step between them to make sure he can't get near her again.

The guy drawls something in a slurred undertone. I can't understand a word he says. He tries to take a step toward me and buckles to the floor on the spot.

A bunch of other people pull away from him to give him space at the same time that different people move in to remove the guy. He can't even support himself well enough to stand up.

I stay where I am until the onlookers go back to their own business. I finally turn around to face Allison. "Are you okay?"

Before she can answer, something flies out of nowhere, clubs me across the eyebrow, and knocks me to the ground. I have half a second to recognize Clay before he hauls off and kicks me in the head.

Allison shoots off her chair and tries to grab his arm, but he shoves her away too hard and sends her staggering against the bar.

I try to get up to help her, but my head won't stop spinning. He pounces on me, punches me hard into the floor five or six times, and then stands up to kick me in the face and body.

"You son of a bitch!" he rages. "You stay the hell away from her! Do you hear me?! Don't you ever come near her again or I swear I'll kill you!"

I huddle under the rain of blows, and in a second, the security guards show up to haul Clay out of the establishment.

I'm too dazed to move. My brother and my friend rush over to me and try to turn me over. "Lie still, man!" Amos tells me. "We're calling an ambulance."

I try to look around. "Allison....."

"Who's Allison?" Buck asks.

I swim into semi-consciousness, and the next thing I know, Carter is bending over me. "Easy, man," he tells me. "Don't try to move. We're taking you in for a head CT."

I couldn't move if I tried. I try to cooperate when they load me onto a gurney. I can't believe this is happening to me. I'm a patient in my own ambulance.

I try not to think or even be alive on the ride to the hospital. My head is killing me.

I drift into a haze inside the CT machine. I actually regret it when they take me out and tell me there's no permanent damage and I can go home.

Buck and Amos stand up from their waiting room chairs when they see me limping down the hospital corridor toward them.

Luckily for me, two Police officers step out of nowhere just then to intercept me. "We need to take statements from all three of you about the incident."

"You'll excuse me if I sit down for this," I mumble and sink into one of the chairs.

Buck and Amos remain standing and tell the whole sorry tale. They don't know who Clay and Allison are. Buck and Amos think she was just some random hotty who caught my eye in a bar.

Things turn biblical when my turn comes to tell my story. "So you never saw the guy before?" one of the officers asked. "He just attacked you out of nowhere for no reason?"

I take a deep breath. "No, I know who he is."

"Who is he?"

I heave an almighty sigh before I can bring myself to say the rest. "His name is Clay Wescott. He's an orthopedic surgeon at the hospital. The girl is his fiancé—Allison Metcalfe. She's a paramedic at Howe Firehouse. We work together. He thinks I was hitting on her when I was only trying to protect her from some drunk guy who was harassing her."

The officers don't think anything about this. "We have the assailant in custody. He's being charged with aggravated assault and for making threats against your life. Twenty witnesses from the bar saw the whole fight and heard him saying he would kill you."

"It wasn't a fight," Amos interjects. "Caleb never even raised his hands to defend himself against the guy. It was completely one-sided."

The officer nods. "That's what the other witnesses say. We have all the statements on record and security camera footage from the bar. All the evidence will be presented to the defendant and-or his attorney. He'll probably plead guilty and get out on bail pending sentencing. You might want to think about getting a restraining order."

I snort under my breath. I feel too rotten even to answer.

No way in hell will I get a restraining order against a pansy like Clay Wescott. I didn't see him coming that time. He hit me down before I realized what was happening.

I won't be so forgiving next time. If he ever tries anything with me again, he'll be the one taking a trip to the hospital and he won't get released after only a simple head CT.

Chapter 8: Allison

I cringe on the hard, plastic chair in the Police Station waiting room and rub my hands up and down my arms.

What the hell am I even doing here?

Drunks, drug addicts, toothless homeless people, and a few normal-looking people slouch, snore, and doze in the chairs around me.

This place smells like a stale combination of ancient tobacco smoke, even older urine, and the acrid stench of unwashed human bodies.

I'm the only person in here wearing clean clothes. Four hours have passed since Clay got arrested. That's enough time for me to go home and change out of the clothes I wore to the bar.

I knew when I put on that dress that I would get a lot of unwanted attention from other men—strange men.

Clay wanted me to dress up for him. He wanted to show me off and impress everyone with how hot I am—or some ridiculous nonsense like that.

I'm also the only person awake in this waiting room. It's four o'clock in the morning and I have to be back at the firehouse in three hours. How did my life come to this?

I clamp my eyes shut in shame when I remember the incident at the bar. I can't stop thinking about the look of rabid fury on Clay's face when he stood up straight and smashed his boot heel into Caleb's face.

I've never met a nicer guy than Caleb. Caleb never did anything to deserve getting beaten and kicked like that.

He was trying to help me. Of course he was. He has never done anything else—ever.

I used to think Clay was the nicest guy I've ever met. Now I know differently.

He turned into a monster when he attacked Caleb—just like Clay turned into a monster when he cornered me in the hospital supply room.

What in God's name is happening to me? I moved here to marry the man of my dreams—or so I thought. Now he's turning into a violent psycho and I'm sitting in the Police station waiting room waiting to bail him out on aggravated assault charges.

A door slams somewhere and startles me into jumping in my chair. No one else in the waiting room stirs from their slumber.

I spin around and wilt in relief when I see James Rooney, the bail bondsman. He enters the waiting room and wedges himself into the seat next to me.

"Well, your fiancé just posted bail," he tells me. "He'll be coming out of the jail release portal in fifteen minutes."

"Thank you," I mumble. "I never thought I'd ever have to deal with someone like you."

He only smiles at me. "That's how it is in our profession. No one wants to know we exist until they need us." He hands me a manila envelope. "Here's all the information on your fiancé's hearing date. If he doesn't show up, the bond will be forfeit and a warrant will be issued for his arrest."

"I got that. Thank you."

He smiles at me. "You know, I don't usually say things like this to people like you—but then again, I don't usually see people like you in my line of work."

I look away. "Go ahead and say it. I really need to hear it right now."

"Maybe....just maybe....you should take steps to ensure that something like this doesn't happen again. I'm just saying." He gets up. "I wish you all the best and I hope I never see you again."

He walks out of the waiting room. Of course he's right. I never should have let myself get into this situation.

I didn't know I was getting into this situation. I never would have believed Clay could be capable of something like this.

I never thought he would be capable of scaring me the way he did in the hospital supply room, either. I never thought I would ever get involved with anyone who would ever scare me—for any reason.

I've always considered myself too good for that. I've always considered someone scaring their partner is the first and last non-negotiable dealbreaker.

Is that what I've come to? Am I really ready to break up with Clay over the incident in the supply room—and the fact that he beat up Caleb? Is this a dealbreaker or not?

It should be. A smart woman would have walked away after that incident in the supply room.

I should have told him then and there that we were over just based on the way he was acting.

He scared me. I actually thought he was going to hurt me—or at least that he was capable of it. Isn't that enough?

I stand up, walk out of the Police Station, and walk around the building. I have to get directions from another officer before I find the release portal. Then I have to stand around for another ten minutes and wait for Clay to come out.

God only knows what I'm going to say to him.

I should break up with him. I should tell him right now that we're over, but I already know I won't say that.

Is this what abused women go through? Is this how they get frozen and incapable of leaving even when they know they should?

I'm not an abused woman. Clay hasn't raised a finger against me, but what difference does that make?

He's violent. I know that now.

How long will it take before he turns against me, too? In a way, he already has turned against me.

I see him long before he gets out. The officers inside the gate let him into a holding area, search him, talk to him for a minute, and then let him into another holding area.

They have to open and close each gate in front of him and behind him before they open the final gate to let him out.

He barges right up to me. "What the hell is wrong with you?" he demands.

I gasp in shock. "What?! What are you talking about?!"

"I'm talking about you encouraging Caleb again right in front of me! What is the matter with you? You really don't give a crap about us, do you? It's all about Caleb!"

"What the hell are you talking about?!" I practically shriek. "I never encouraged Caleb at all—ever!"

"I saw him standing right in front of you, you worthless tramp—after I already told you to stay away from him! I saw him hitting on you at the bar. What the hell did you think—that I was just going to stand by and let him take you away from me without doing anything about it?"

My jaw drops all over again. "He was not hitting on me—and I was not encouraging him! He was trying to protect me from some drunk who tried to kiss me!"

"So now he's the one protecting you instead of me?!" he fires back. "That's just great."

"You weren't even there! You said you had to go to the bathroom. This drunk guy almost fell on top of me. I was all by myself. Caleb couldn't possibly have known that you were there—and I had no idea he was there until he stepped between me and the drunk."

"What—is he following you around town now?"

"No, Clay! What is wrong with you? What is your problem with Caleb? He's my co-worker—that's all!"

"I told you to stay away from him! I told you never to work with him again!"

"I haven't!" I counter. "I haven't worked with him since you told me that. I haven't even seen him before tonight and I had no idea he was at that bar. I never saw him. I never talked to him. You had no right to hit him like that and now you're...."

"Don't you dare tell me what I can and can't do! He horned in between you and me. He's been doing it ever since you started working at the Fire Department."

"He asked me out! That's all! And he dropped it the minute I told him I was with you. He's been nothing but respectful ever since."

"So now you're defending him! You're taking his side against me!"

My blood turns to ice. All my hesitation evaporates and turns to fury. I lower my voice.

We're still standing right outside the gate leading into the Howe County Jail. All the officers can hear us arguing, but I don't give a crap about that anymore.

"You're the one who was out of line tonight, Clay," I snarl. "Caleb did nothing wrong and you attacked him for no reason at all."

"You bitch!" he hisses.

"You're the one who got arrested and put in jail, you moron! You're the one who is being charged with aggravated assault—not him! He never laid a finger on me or you! He never even raised his hand to defend himself—and now you're the one who is going to trial! You're the one who is going to have this on your permanent criminal record for the rest of your life! You're supposed to be a doctor, Clay! What is the matter with you?"

"You know what?" he growls through gritted teeth. "We're finished. We're done. You're a traitorous bitch. I don't give a shit anymore if you sleep with half the county. Go on. You know you want to. I hope you rot in it. I never want to see your face again."

He turns on his heel, walks away, and leaves me standing there stunned.

What in the name of God is going through his head? How can he just have flipped his lid in the last couple of weeks—over nothing?

This isn't the first time other guys have hit on me. I've told him about it.

This is the first time we've lived together in the same town. Maybe someone hitting on me means something different to Clay now.

Maybe our relationship was never real to him before. Maybe someone hitting on him didn't threaten him the way it does now.

None of that excuses his behavior.

One part of me wants to run after him and try to reason with him. I want to convince him that I never encouraged Caleb nor did I ever allow him to think there could be anything between us.

The other part of me—the rational part of me—knows this is right. I should have been the one to break up with Clay. Now he's doing the job for me.

I need to let him. I need to let go of all of this. I need to let him walk out of my life. He's dangerous—to me, to everyone around me, and to himself.

I turn off in the other direction and start walking. I don't know where to go. Clay and I bought a house together in Howe. That's the only place I have left to go.

I could get a motel room for the night, but I have to show up at the firehouse in less than three hours. There's no point in going home, especially not if Clay is going to be there.

I do need to get my uniform and a few other things for my shift. I make up my mind. If he's there, I'll just get my stuff and leave. I'll go to the firehouse early and stay in the bunk room until my shift starts.

If Clay insists on staying in the house, I'll have to move out. I'll stay in a motel room tomorrow until I can find another place to live.

Jesus, what is my life coming to that I actually have to think about these things? I really am thinking like an abused woman escaping a violent relationship.

James Rooney is so right. I can never let this happen again—especially not with Clay. If he wakes up tomorrow or a week from now and regrets the things he said to me, I can never take him back.

I can never take him back no matter what. It's over. It really is over. It has to be.

I start walking back to the Police Station parking lot to get my car, but I wind up walking in the wrong direction. I let my mind drift. I don't even understand what my life is anymore.

I'm a paramedic at Howe Firehouse. That's all I know.....and for some reason, it's enough.

The crew......they're so awesome. They'll understand about all of this. They'll support me....because I'm one of them.

I still have that. The firehouse and the crew—they anchor me to reality. I know who I am and where I belong. Clay doesn't matter anymore.

He was never who I am or where I belong. He was just a passing fancy—a vehicle to get me here so I could find the firehouse.

I walk all the way back to the house—the house I used to share with Clay. Never again.

His car isn't in the driveway. I don't know where he is and I don't really care as long as he isn't here.

I walk in the front door and see right away that he has already come through here before me. He emptied his drawers in the bedroom, took a suitcase out of the closet, and also took his laptop and a few other electronics.

The house looks somehow more forlorn without him in it, but that doesn't matter. I'll stay here as long as I have to until we sell it. I won't keep this house.

This was the house we were supposed to live in as a married couple. We were supposed to raise children in this house. We were going to be so happy in this house.

None of those dreams can come true now.

I go into the bedroom, put a few things back in the closet, put the drawers back into the dresser, and pack my duffel bag for work.

I change into my uniform, put extra uniforms into the duffel bag, and add things I never would take to work otherwise.

I take two changes of casual clothes, my toothbrush and toothpaste, hairbrush and hair products, and I pack my makeup into a makeup kit just in case I don't come back here at all.

God Almighty, am I really thinking this?

I cross a line in my mind. It's over. The past is dead. Everything I shared with Clay over the last two years—all dead. He's gone. I'm gone. It's all gone. He killed it.

I linger for a long time on the threshold to look around the house and remember. I don't have any memories of living in this house with Clay. We never built a life together. That was all just a foolish dream.

I walk out and pull the door closed. I'll come back here as long as Clay stays away.

I don't have to come back here, though. I'll be fine if I never come back or even if I never see this place again.

This house means nothing to me. Everything I hoped it would be is dead. It's just a relic of the past waiting for us to sell it.

I leave the duffel bag on the front porch, walk all the way back to the Police Station, get my car, drive back to the house, pick up my duffel bag, and drive to the firehouse.

Chapter 9: Caleb

I take a deep breath to steady my nerves and groan when I climb out of my pickup.

My head still throbs and my body aches with bruises, but I can't let that stop me from going to work.

I'm not hurt enough for that. I won't let myself be hurt enough for that. I can't let Clay rob me of this.

I hobble into the firehouse garage and immediately get laughed at by Theo, Vince, and Danny. "All hail, the conquering hero!" Vince teases.

"Did you at least put the other guy into a coma?" Theo asks.

I look away and wince again when I feel the pinch in my ribs. "I don't want to talk about it."

"What happened?" Danny asks. "Don't tell me you fell down the stairs again."

I don't look at them. I might glare in smoldering fury if I did.

Just then, Keith and Billy walk around the rescue truck and see me. Keith pretends to jump in horror. "Holy crap, dude! Did you get stuck in the meat grinder?"

The others laugh and then, in my worst nightmare, Jessie, Sophie, and Chris all come over.

"Oh, my God!" Jessie exclaims. "Are you all right?"

"I'm fine," I grumble. "Leave me alone. It's nothing."

"It's a little more than nothing, man," Keith tells me. "What happened?"

I wait for someone else to make a funny quip to deflect them from noticing that I don't answer.

They don't make a funny quip, though. No one says anything. They just stand there waiting for me to answer. It gets worse when Carter comes over just then to join the group.

"What happened?" he asks.

"Yeah," Chris asks. "What happened to your face, Caleb?"

I can't keep it to myself anymore. They crew is going to find out eventually. I have to take it on the chin.

"I was at the bar last night playing pool with my boys.....and I saw some drunk hitting on Allison...."

"Not Allison again," Keith snarls.

"I thought she was alone. I didn't see her man around and this drunk guy tried to kiss her and almost fell on top of her. I just stepped in to tell the guy to back off...."

"Did he kick the shit out of you?" Billy asks. "You couldn't beat a drunk guy?"

"Her fiancé did it!" I blurt out. "I didn't even know he was in the bar! I just got the drunk guy away from her and her fiancé came out of nowhere and hit me in the face. He knocked me down and started kicking me all over....."

A hushed gasp falls over the group. "That's awful!" Sophie exclaims. "I'm so sorry, Caleb!"

I look away. "Her fiancé got arrested. That's all you need to know."

"Damn," Keith murmurs. "That's not good."

"Can we drop it and get back to work? I'm fine."

I turn away to the locker room. This is the last thing in the world I want to talk about—now or ever.

"Hey, did you hear about the new...." Billy begins and immediately breaks off.

I look up at him and notice him and all the others staring at something behind me. I glance over my shoulder and my blood runs cold when I see Allison standing there.

She sees my battered face and then she sees everyone staring at her.

I can't deal with her, so I walk away to the locker room and put my stuff away. I hear the others talking to her out in the garage. Now I have to go out there so I can start work.

I'm rostered on the rescue truck with her today, too. This couldn't get any worse.

I plan to go out there and bury myself in my truck checks so I don't have to deal with her, but she ambushes me before I get out of the locker room.

She stops in the doorway and stares at me. Now I can't get out of here.

She gulps, walks toward me, and drops her duffel bag on the bench next to me. "I'm really sorry about last night," she murmurs. "I'm really sorry you got mixed up in the middle of all of this. You didn't deserve that at all. I'm really grateful to you for trying to help me—and I'm really grateful for how respectful and considerate you've been toward me since I started working here. You've been a total prince since day one, so thank you."

I look away. I can't stand the way she looks at me with such care and concern.

"Yeah, well, I guess someone had to do it, didn't they?" I mumble for no reason. "I didn't know your man was in the bar. I wouldn't have intervened if I had known."

"I know! I know you only did it to help me—and I'm grateful for that. I'm just really sorry—about everything.....Are you all right?"

I twiddle with my locker so I don't have to look at her. "Yeah, I'm fine....I mean...not really, but I'll make it."

"Clay and I split up last night," she tells me. "He couldn't let it go and he still thinks there's something going on between us. He doesn't believe me when I tell him there isn't, so he dumped me. I'm only telling you this because I want you to know he won't cause you any problems from now on. He's out of my life, so he has no reason to feel jealous of you."

"It's probably for the best," I remark. "For you, I mean. You don't need a guy like that around."

"Yeah," she murmurs. "I know."

I find myself looking at her. I suppose I have no reason to stop myself from caring about her. She's my crewmate. I can care about her the same way I care about the others.

"What will you do?" I ask. "Will you move back to Woodhurst...or wherever it is you came from?"

"I don't know." She looks away. "I have to figure it out, but I'm in no hurry to leave this job. It's pretty nice here and I really like the people. I'll stay here until I figure it out." She turns around and smiles at me. "The good news is we can both put this behind us and go back to work. I really enjoy working with you. I hope we can just continue with that and forget about all of this."

I nod. "Okay. That sounds good."

We both walk out of the locker room and head for the garage. We split up and start doing our truck checks, but we do them separately.

The rest of the crew pretends like the incident never happened, too. Duke comes in mid-morning and takes me up to his office to demand an explanation for why my face is a mass of bruises.

I tell him the story, but I also tell him what Allison just told me downstairs. It's over between her and Clay, which means it's over between me and Clay, too.

The whole thing is over for all of us, so we can all move on with the rest of our lives.

We finish the shift without incident. I leave and head home for the night. I don't even consider going out even though I have the next two days off from work.

I just plan to crawl into bed and stay there for the entire weekend—except maybe to get out for food and go to the bathroom.

That's as much as I can handle right now—and I'm putting an absolute moratorium on all drama. I'm closed for business where any kind of drama is concerned.

I turn onto the highway to head for the other side of Howe. I'm just starting to relax when a low, tight BMW roadster speeds alongside me driving way too fast.

I don't see the driver through the tinted side windows, but he must be doing at least a hundred and fifty.

He whizzes past me, dodges between two cars, swerves back into the other lane, and races off into the distance.

I actually slow down to make sure I don't get anywhere near him. He can go kill himself somewhere else.

I drive another minute and a half before I almost collide with a massive wreck in the middle of the road.

A bunch of other cars stop and block traffic from getting through. My pickup is three cars behind the blockade.

I jump out, grab the emergency kit from behind my seat, and charge out there. A bunch of people are already on their phones calling the 911 dispatcher.

Three cars lie overturned across all four lanes of the highway. The BMW roadster lies on its roof not far away.

The nearest car has its driver window open. A woman hangs upside down from her seatbelt in the driver's seat and I hear kids screaming and crying in the back.

I rush over there and flatten myself to the pavement to lean through the window. "I'm a firefighter with the Fire Department, Ma'am!" I tell her. "Look at me! Are you injured anywhere?"

She bawls her eyes out with tears streaming down her cheeks. "He ran into us! He was driving too fast and he ran us off the road!"

"I know, Ma'am! I know it wasn't your fault! Look at me! Are you hurt anywhere? I'm going to get you out?"

Her terrified eyes swivel in my direction. She's crying too hard to speak.

"Are you hurt anywhere?" I ask again. "Can you get out and walk?"

"My children!" she wails. "My children!"

"I'm going to get them out, too!" I see my words bouncing right off her, so I take a chance and glance into the back.

Three children sit buckled into their car seats—also upside down. They're all screaming, but they don't look hurt.

I open the rear passenger door and start taking them out one at a time.

"You're gonna be okay," I tell the first one. He's a boy about four years old. "You're all right. I'm with the Fire Department. We're getting you out."

As I suspected, seeing me handling her children brings the mother out of it. She takes off her seatbelt, falls on her head, and then crawls out through the driver's window.

She gathers her children just as I take out the third child.

I push all of them toward the barricade of cars. "Go over there. Get away from the wreck."

Chapter 10: Caleb

I go to the next wrecked car. The driver is a man in a business suit with his face and head completely pulverized.

I don't dare to touch him. I leave him for the paramedics to handle. This is way above my training to cope with.

A woman equally badly injured sits in the passenger seat. I glance into the rear to make sure they don't have any other passengers. Then I go to the third car other than the roadster.

The roadster driver is the least of my priorities right now. He's the one who did all this. He can damn well wait.

The driver and passengers of the third car are another family and they are also walking wounded. I help them get out just as the fire trucks and ambulances arrive.

The Police direct them up the shoulder to park adjacent to the scene. I go over there to talk to Duke and the paramedics about what I've been doing and to report on the critical patients who are left.

I get halfway to Duke when a puff of wind blows the smell of gasoline to my nostrils. I glance over my shoulder and see a clear fluid dripping from the roadster. It dribbles down the fender to form a puddle on the ground....and bursts into flame there.

I don't wait around to see what's causing it to burn. I charge back to the roadster and dart around to the driver's door.

I yank it open.....and stop dead in my tracks when I see Clay hanging from the seatbelt. Blood drips from his forehead and he's out cold.

He's the one who did this. He's the one who put two families in danger with his reckless driving and might even have killed two other people.

I can't believe it, but I have no choice but to accept the evidence of my own eyes.

Right then, I catch another whiff of gasoline. As if by magic, flames shoot up the other side of the car. They crawl up the fender where I just saw gas running across the car's outer body.

I dive into the driver's compartment and attack Clay's seatbelt in a frenzy. The buckle won't unclip no matter how hard I yank it.

I snatch my multitool from my belt, open the blade, slash the seatbelt, and haul him out of the seat. I don't have time to be careful or to protect his neck in case he hurt himself.

I get him three feet away from the car before the whole thing detonates in my face. I spin around, fling my body over him, grab him, and roll the rest of the way to safety just as Danny, Duke, and Josh make it over to me.

They pull me and Clay away from the wreck and Josh starts patting me down all over. "Did you get hurt anywhere?!" he yells at me over the whoof of flames.

"I'm okay!" I gasp. "I'm okay!"

"Lie still while I check you out." He does a full physical exam.

By the time he finishes, the other paramedics have Clay loaded onto a gurney. He's conscious now and I hear him talking to the paramedics and firefighters as they load him into the ambulance.

I stay where I am and watch the crew extricate the two critical patients, treat them, and transport them, too.

The Police stand across the scene interviewing the passengers I helped earlier. No doubt they're giving the Police an earful about how Clay ran them off the road.

Duke comes over to me just then. "You okay, man?" he asks. "Josh is giving you a clean bill of health."

"I'm fine," I mutter out the side of my mouth. "Don't ask me why I saved that piece of shit."

He claps me on the shoulder. "Go sit down by the rescue truck. Take a load off. You've done your good deed for the day."

I do as he says. I couldn't get my truck out of the traffic jam right now anyway.

I just want to sit somewhere and stop thinking. I don't want to think about the fact that I just saved Clay's life when he recklessly endangered so many other people.

I could have died in that wreck, too. I could have been one of the cars he clipped and caused to crash.

Those two critical patients might not even survive. Then he'll be charged with vehicular homicide on top of whatever charges he'll face for reckless driving and endangerment.

I'm still sitting there pretending not to think about that when the woman and her three children come over to me.

The woman sobs her eyes out and hugs her children tight to her body. "Thank you...so much....I can't thank you enough...." she gushes. "God Bless you—whoever you are...."

"It's all right," I mumble. "I was just doing my job. I'm just glad you're all okay."

Duke stands off to one side and watches while the three kids come forward to hug me one after the other. They all thank me.

"Thank you, Mister," the little boy tells me.

I have to smile at him. "My name's Caleb. You can call me that."

"Thank you, Caleb," he repeats.

"You're welcome, buddy. You take care of your mom and your sisters, okay?" I smile up at the rest of them. "I'm glad you're okay."

Just then, the same two Police officers from the hospital come over. They talk to Duke first. "We need to take his statement if he's up to it."

I stand up to face them and the mother and her children make themselves scarce.

Duke stays next to me while I tell the officers what happened—first about the roadster passing me at high speed and then finding the same car wrecked over there.

They take it all in stride. They must have heard the same thing from all the witnesses.

Duke listens in silence until I finish, He's still standing there when the officers leave me alone.

"Don't say it," I growl. "Don't say I did wrong by helping those people or even pulling that jackass out of the car before it blew up."

"I wasn't going to say that," he murmurs. "I was going to say that you're one of the finest firefighters I've ever worked with. I admire you for what you did here today—especially because of your history with him. That makes what you did truly exceptional. I'm proud to serve on the same crew with you. You deserve a decoration for what you did here today."

I look away. "I don't want one."

"Commendations like that go on your permanent record. They count toward promotions and salary increases. Take it in good grace. You earned it by being a hero. If you don't believe me, just ask those kids over there. I'm sure they agree with me that you should be decorated for this."

I don't know what to say, so I don't say anything.

The patients are all gone. The Police section off one lane of traffic to get the roadblock out of the way. The first cars start to file past.

The vehicle accident forensics team is already going through the scene taking millions of pictures and marking off the distance between cars and skid marks.

There's nothing more to see here and the Police tell me to move my truck. I get into it and continue driving home. Now I can put this whole sorry episode behind me and stop thinking for the next forty-eight hours.

Chapter 11: Allison

I go through the house and pack all of Clay's stuff in boxes. I don't want any delays when he decides to move out of here.

I still haven't decided what to do with my own life. I only know we'll sell this house. I've already listed it with the same real estate agent who sold it to us.

I use the same packing boxes to gather up my own stuff—starting with the non-essentials. I keep out anything I need for work, kitchen gear—all that stuff.

I'll have to move out of this house eventually, too. I've already started looking for an apartment to rent until I decide whether to stay in Howe or move back to....somewhere else.

I go into the garage. Both Clay and I have a ton of stuff stored in here. I don't even know where to start, but right then, my phone rings.

I stiffen when I see that the call is from Clay.

I answer it fully prepared to deliver an epic smackdown. I don't want to talk to this fool ever again.

The farther I get from that moment of truth outside the Police Station, the more certain I become that breaking up with him is the best thing for me.

I just need to make sure nothing like this ever happens again, especially not with him.

I answer the phone. "Hello?"

"Allison—you gotta help me!" he blurts out on the other end. "I don't know who else to call! You have to help me! You're my last hope."

I roll my eyes to Heaven. "What do you want?"

"You have to bail me out of jail! Whatever you did last time, you have to do it again. You have to get me out of here."

I groan in exasperation. "What is it this time? Did you get into another fight?"

"No, I got into a wreck on the highway. I hit a couple of other cars....and I'm being charged with reckless endangerment....and one count of vehicular homicide. You have to help me, Allison! I can't stay in here. You don't know what it's like! The detectives in charge of the case are saying they're going for a no-bail hearing and I'll be sent to prison upstate even before I go to trial! You can't leave me in here!"

I stare into space at nothing as those words sink in. Vehicular homicide?

He must have been doing a lot more than just driving down the highway. He must have done something really bad—something a lot worse than just having a random accident.

"Are you there?" His voice trembles. Is he about to start crying? "You can't leave me in here, Allison. I love you. I made a terrible mistake—about all of it. Caleb.....he pulled me out of my car and saved my life...right before flames hit the gas tank and the car exploded.....I didn't realize what a great guy he is....I'm so sorry....about everything I said...about you....and him.....and everything.....Give me another chance. You can't let me go to prison, Allision. We have something special. You know we do. Don't throw all that away."

I clamp my lips shut to stop myself from telling him that he was the one who threw it all away.

I can't go back. I can't get back together with him even if he did have a change of heart.

I think fast. "We still have the money in our joint checking account," I tell him. "Half of it is yours. I'll use that to bail you out."

"Thank you so much!" he chokes. "I love you more than anything. I can't wait to see you."

I get off the phone as quickly and politely as possible. Then I call James Rooney. He looks up the case on his computer.

"The bail amount is half a million dollars," he tells me.

I almost scream in shock. "Jesus Christ!"

"So ten percent of that would be fifty thousand. Do you think you can come up with that?"

I run through a few mental calculations. "I think so. I'll take out a lien on the house and then get it back from his share when we sell. I'll see you in a few hours."

I pay a visit to the bank. I still have good credit, so I take out the lien, get the money, and deliver it to James Rooney.

He in turn pays a visit to the jail and posts Clay's bail.

I don't sit around in the Police Department waiting room. To hell with that. Life is too short.

I wait at home until James calls me and tells me that Clay is being released. I take my time driving over there. Let the bastard wait for me for a change.

I park in the parking lot, walk over to the gate, and find him waiting there. He rushes toward me way too fast. "Oh, thank God you're here!" he gushes. "Thank you so much! I love you...."

I straight-arm him away from me. "Stop right there. We are not getting back together. Back off and don't touch me."

He blinks at me in disbelief. What a moron. "What? Why not? I thought...."

"Why not?!" I snap back. "Why not? Because you're a raving asshole, Clay. You're a violent, uncontrollable, murdering, psychopathic piece of shit. That's why. You threatened me in the supply room at the hospital when you thought there was something going on between me and Caleb and there wasn't."

"I told you I changed my mind about that."

"And that somehow makes it okay for you to get in my face and threaten me for no reason? Then you beat the shit out of an innocent man at the bar, got yourself arrested, and now you're charged with ten counts of reckless endangerment plus vehicular homicide. What did you do, Clay? What were you doing when you crashed your car?"

He opens his mouth, but no sound comes out. So I was right. He did do something bad. Of course he did. He wouldn't be getting charged if he didn't.

"You are everything I try to avoid in a man, Clay—and let's not forget that you were the one who dumped me. You dumped me over this whole stupid Caleb bullshit when I told you a million times that nothing was going on. So don't think you can say you love me and waltz back into my life. It's over. I'm selling the house....."

He gasps. "You can't sell the house! Half of it is mine."

"Oh, and by the way, I took out a lien on your half of the house to pay your bail just now, so when we sell it, you'll be reimbursing me for fifty thousand dollars out of your share. Got that?"

His mouth falls open. "Fifty thousand?!"

"The total bail amount was half a million, so consider yourself lucky. I put the house on the market..."

"But where will I live if you sell the house? I got fired from my job at the hospital over all of this. I have nowhere to go."

I take a fraction of an instant to take that in, too. This is the final straw. He really is the ultimate loser.

I throw up my hands. "Where you live isn't my concern anymore. We're finished. I'm staying in the house until it sells. You can come by and pick up your stuff as soon as you make arrangements to move it somewhere. Don't come around asking me to get back together. Don't call me unless it's some legal matter related to the sale. You'll be hearing from the realtor as soon as she has some papers for you to sign to finalize the sale. I already removed my name from our joint bank account and I already informed our mortgage officer that we won't be making any future payments on the mortgage. The bank can take the balance of the mortgage out of the sale price—and I've already filed a petition with the real estate escrow office to have the bail amount reimbursed to me out of the sale price, too. As far as I'm concerned, all our business together is concluded. We have nothing more to say to each other. I really hope you pull your life together. Clay, but as far as I'm concerned, it doesn't really affect me anymore if you do or you don't. Good luck."

I turn around and walk off. Good riddance. I should have said all that a long time ago.

I walk back to my car, drive to the house, and go straight back to packing. Now I know for certain that I'm out of here. I don't know where I'll go or what I'll do, but I definitely won't stay here.

The past is dead and buried—as it should be.

Chapter 12: Caleb

I raise my head and listen when I hear a car door slam out in my driveway. I'm all alone in my house, sprawled on the couch in my sweatpants and hoodie, and watching reruns of *MASH* while I eat potato chips out of the bag.

I don't even care that I'm getting crumbs all over the couch and floor. I'm slumming it here. I deserve it after the week I just had.

I mute the TV and sit up when I hear footsteps coming up the steps to my porch. I get to my feet, turn around, and almost have a heart attack when I see Clay stopping to knock on my door.

I take a minute to brush the crumbs off my hoodie—like I give a shit what this idiot thinks of me.

I pull the door open and glare at him across the threshold. "Can I help you?"

He squirms all over the place. He looks as good as ever—only not so self-possessed. He can't stop shuffling his feet. "Look, you gotta help me!" he blurts out. "I know I don't have any right to ask you this...."

"Ask me what?"

"You gotta help me get Allison back!" he chokes. "She won't have anything to do with me. She dumped me....."

"Really? She said you dumped her."

"That was before....before the whole accident thing......"

I raise my eyebrows. "Accident thing? Is that what you're calling it? I heard one of the patients died on the operating table. I hope you're happy, man."

"Just listen to me, all right?! I'm going crazy! I didn't realize....I'm sorry.....I didn't realize what a great guy you are.....and then.....the paramedics in the ambulance told me.....they told me that you were the one who pulled me out of the car......"

I look away and snort. "You're making me regret that now."

"Please!" he husks. "Please help me get her back. I know I screwed up.....with you.....and everything.....and I know I shouldn't have accused you......"

"I never did anything with her, pal," I counter. "Let's just be clear about that right now. I asked her out, but that was before I knew she was with you. I dropped it the minute I found out she was with you. I never looked sideways at her after that."

"I know that!" he quavers. "I'm sorry! I wish I could take it all back, but I have to find a way to make up with her."

"Try not being such an asshole next time."

I hear myself being extra harsh, but I don't feel like taking it easy on him. He damn well killed someone on the highway and now he has the nerve to come crawling to me for help?

He might have a medical license, but this chump doesn't have the brains God gave a goose.

"Will you at least talk to her for me, man?" he begs. "Please? I lost my job at the hospital over this whole thing...."

Good. I don't say it, but I'm thinking it. This dipshit has no business being responsible for the wellbeing of others.

"Now she's selling our house and dividing the money.....and I have nowhere to live...."

"What exactly do you want me to do?" I ask. "What exactly do you want me to say to her—because, I'll be honest here, I already told her I think you two breaking up is the best thing for her. I still think that."

"Just talk to her. I don't care what you say to her. She trusts you. She'll listen to you."

I don't know if Allison trusts me or if she'll listen to me. If she does, telling her to get back together with this idiot would be the worst thing I could do for her.

I would never do that to one of my crewmates. We're family. We look out for each other. We have each other's backs.

We help each other out of situations just like this. Keith took a bullet in the head trying to protect Leila from an out-of-control psycho exactly like this piece of shit standing in front of me right now.

That's what I call a man. That's the example I try to live up to every day —the Brewer brothers. They would never let any woman they respect get back together with this waste of oxygen.

I respect Allison. She's a member of our crew and part of the firehouse family. I would do anything to protect her from harm.

No way in hell could I ever use whatever small influence I have with her to convince her to get back together with this.....this murderer.

That's what he is. This man in front of me is a murderer. He killed someone by being a lowlife, reckless, violent prick.

Any of those kids could have gotten killed in that wreck. Mothers and fathers could have gotten killed in that wreck.

The dead guy had a wife and kids. Clay left them widowed and fatherless. That's the creep who is asking me to put him back together with a high-quality woman like Allison.

I don't have the heart to tell him so to his face. I should, but I'm not one to kick a man when he's down. He's already getting kicked by life and society.

He'll get convicted of vehicular homicide and go away to prison for a long time. Then the other inmates will kick him enough for all of us. Maybe then he'll learn something.

His features twitch and spasm when he stands in front of me. This.....this boy.....this overgrown child.....he doesn't even have the brains to grieve for the man he killed. Clay doesn't care about anyone but himself. He really does belong in prison.

"So....will you help me?" he chokes. "Will you at least talk to her for me?"

I take a deep breath. "I'll talk to her about it. I can't promise anything, but I'll talk to her."

He lunges for me and grabs my hand. "Thank you so much! You're the best! I can't thank you enough! I owe you big time for this. Thank you!"

He steps back, thank God, clasps his own hands together in something like prayer, beams at me, and then races back to his car. Heaven only knows where he got it after he wrecked his roadster on the highway.

He waves to me, bursts into another big grin, calls, "Thank you so much!" again, and drives away.

I stand on the porch watching him out of sight. Don't ask me what I'm going to say to Allision, but I know one thing.

I won't try to talk her into getting back together with Clay. That is the absolute last thing I would ever say to her.

I go back to my Couch of Doom, but I can't get interested in watching TV—or in defiling myself with junk food.

I need to think and take my mind off this at the same time, so I go to firehouse gym and do a really hard workout.

I have to go back to work tomorrow anyway, so I spend the rest of the day running errands, doing chores around the house, vacuuming up all the potato chip crumbs, and getting my life in order.

I don't want to become another Clay. I want to stay on the straight and narrow the way I have been these last several years.

I want to look at my life and know that I'm doing the right thing as much as possible.

I only have to look at the Brewer brothers to see the right path. All I have to do is follow their example and try to be as good a man as each of them.

I don't hold out any hope of being as good as John or Keith, but I might be as good as Danny if I really try.

He used to be such a single young stud. Every woman lusted after him and he had more decorations than the rest of the crew combined.

Now he's married with a stepson and one of his own on the way. If Danny can pull his life together like that, so can I.

He had Keith and John to guide him and show him what to do—and so do I. They're the big brothers I never had. Amos never set that example for me and neither did my dad.

Someday I might get to be as heroic and responsible as the Brewer brothers. I can only hope.

I go to bed early, go to the firehouse early, and do another workout. Keith, Billy, Carter, and Ellis are all already there. We work out together. Hell yeah. This is what it's all about.

Ellis doesn't talk to any of us, but he works out just as hard and works up a sweat. Carter works out with his shirt off. None of us pay the slightest attention to his scars anymore. The guy is an animal, plain and simple.

We finish before the shift starts, go upstairs, take showers in the bunk room bathroom, and get into our uniforms.

We're all downstairs ready to roll when the clock strikes seven and the night crew comes downstairs to go off shift.

Allison is rostered on the rescue truck. I'm rostered on the ladder truck, so I don't have any problem avoiding her. I still don't know what to say to her, but I can't say anything to her when the rest of the crew is around.

We finish our truck checks. After that, we have a staff meeting with Duke where we talk about nothing but the roster. The discussion goes on and on and doesn't really come to any conclusion.

"So what you're saying is that we can't resolve any of these issues until we hire new staff," Keith finishes. "That's basically the gist of it, isn't it? We just don't have enough people, so the roster is going to keep being a problem until you hire on some new people."

Duke cocks his head to one side and then nods. "Yeah. That pretty much sums it up. I've been advertising—but you already know how John was advertising for years before I came on. We hired Allison and I'll keep hiring good people as they come up, but there isn't a lot I can do before then. We'll all just have to work with it as best we can."

That ends the meeting—as if we didn't all already know that. We didn't need to spend an hour and a half arguing about it.

We head for the breakroom where the usual discussion ensues along with jokes and laughter. I stay on the opposite side of the room from Allison and keep busy talking to other people so she won't feel tempted to engage with me.

We spend the whole day at the firehouse. We don't get one single call all day.

I take my gear out of my locker after work and make my escape. That's another day down when I didn't have to deal with someone else's drama. How much longer can I keep ducking it before I have no choice but to deal with it?

I find out when I head to my truck and Allison comes rushing out of the firehouse to catch up with me. "Caleb!" she calls and pulls up in front of me. "Wait up a sec."

I can't deny anymore that she ran out here just to see me. She isn't carrying her own gear, so she couldn't have been on her way to her car to leave for the evening.

"Hey!" she pants. "I was hoping to talk to you, but I didn't get a chance to earlier."

"Here I am," I tell her. Is she about to tell me that she's getting back together with Clay?

"I wanted to ask you....if you want to go out sometime," she blurts out. "We could go play minigolf—or ride the go-karts—or go to the arcade—or whatever. What do you say?"

I take a deep breath. "I don't think that's a good idea. I'm really flattered, but I have to say no."

Her face falls. "Why? You asked me out before. I'm not with Clay anymore. We're both single...." She grins at me. "Unless some other lucky girl got to you first."

"No one got to me first....unless you count Clay. He came over to my place yesterday and asked me to intervene between you two and help him get back together with you."

Her eyes fall out of their sockets—and then narrow in fury just as fast. "He did not."

I nod. "He got all contrite and pathetic about it and apologized for being such a cocksucker to both of us."

She compresses her mouth. "You didn't tell him you would do it, did you? You didn't tell him you would help us get back together—because I will never get back together with him—not ever! The son of a bitch! How dare he after everything he's done?!"

"I didn't tell him that. I told him I would talk to you—which I am."

"That lowlife bastard!" she snarls and then shakes her hair back. "I will never get back together with him! If he ever mentions it to you again, you can tell him I said so."

"I'm not going to tell him anything. I'm not going to become a carrier pigeon between the two of you flying messages back and forth. If he asks me, I'll say I talked to you—which is the truth. What happens after that is between you two."

"Well, he can forget it. Will you go out with me now?"

I raise both hands. "Sorry, but I can't get involved in this. You just went through a disastrous breakup with a violent criminal. Your life is too chaotic right now. I appreciate that you like me, but you were with Clay for a long time and you're too close to this to think clearly."

"I won't get back together with him!" she snaps. "I will never get back together with him—ever!"

"Okay, I believe you. Just get your life straightened out. Put this whole thing behind you and get clear of it. You might decide that you don't want to stay in Howe and that you want to move away. Figure out your own business before you jump into another relationship with someone you barely know."

She opens her mouth to contradict—probably to tell me that she won't move away from Howe.

She stops herself, though, and I read the truth in that silence. She still doesn't know if she even wants to stay in Howe. She doesn't know whether she's coming or going.

"I gotta go," I tell her. "I enjoy working with you and I know you enjoy working with me. Let's just stick with that for now. You concentrate on getting your life back. That's the best thing you can do right now."

I get into my truck. She's still standing there when I drive away.

Maybe I shouldn't have been so harsh with her, either, but I can't afford to take it easy on either of them.

She's in no state to go out with anyone. She won't be for a long time—not until she puts all of this behind her.

I don't need a woman like that in my life right now—or ever. I need someone on the straight and narrow just like me. I need someone who is ready to have something serious.

I don't want to get all tangled up with a woman who is all tangled up with someone else.

Chapter 13: Allison

I skid my tires on the pavement when I pull up in front of the motel where the real estate agent told me Clay is staying pending the sale of the house.

I get there just as he is heading for his new car. It's a Prius. Ha. That should take him down a peg. He isn't driving fancy sports cars the way he did when he was a bigshot doctor.

I park my car and barge over to him. "What's this bullshit about you setting up Caleb to get us back together?" I demand. "What the hell are you doing asking him of all people to help you get back together with me?"

"I had to do something," he counters. "You wouldn't listen to me and you blocked my phone. I couldn't call you....."

"I told you not to call me!" I rage. "I told you not to try to get back together with me! What part of that did you not understand? What part did you not understand when I said we had nothing more to say to each other?"

"Just hear me out," he stammers. "We can work this out...."

"There is nothing to work out, Clay! We're done! I will never get back together with you. You blew it. You had me living in your house and sleeping in your bed and you threw all of that down the shithole. Do you get that? You destroyed our relationship! You threw me out of your life! You were the one who told me it was over—and don't give me that sob story about how you changed your mind! You don't get to change your mind about being a righteous prick to me, beating up an innocent man and sending another to the morgue, and then come crawling back making a bunch of pathetic excuses! You beat the shit out of Caleb—and he still had the balls to save your worthless life! And this is the man you go asking for help to clean up your mess?! You're a lowlife piece of shit, Clay—and you don't even know what a piece of shit you are! You think you're some kind of prize that a woman would want to get back together with! You're nothing! You're worse than nothing! You're toxic! You're violent! You threatened me! You don't deserve to be in a relationship with any woman—much less me!"

"Aw, come on," he chides. "You don't have to get like that. We can talk about this."

I open my mouth to go off on him again, but just as I start to inhale, I realize that he won't listen. If he didn't hear everything I just said, he won't be able to hear anything. He's completely deaf to reason.

I need to hurt him. I need to break him so he realizes it's over.

My mind latches onto the one thing I know will really push him away from me forever.

"You know what?" I tell him. "I don't need you anymore. I hooked up with Caleb and he's everything you aren't. I hope you're satisfied. You don't need to call me anymore or try to get back together with me. I'm moving on. I don't need you or want you anymore. I have someone else—someone much better."

Clay's expression changes in the blink of an eye. He turns back into the raging monster from the hospital supply room and the bar.

"You filthy rotten bitch!" he snarls. "I knew it all along."

I cross my arms across my chest and wait. This asshole can't say or do anything to hurt me.

"I'll get you for this," he snarls through his teeth. "I'll get you both for this."

"You won't get anyone for anything, you piece of trash," I tell him. "You're going to prison. I hope you have a really nice time there. You deserve it."

He curls his lips back from his teeth in a feral snarl. "You bitch! This isn't over. You'll see."

He spins away, gets in his car, and revs the engine. I have to move out of the way when he skids out of his parking place and drives off. Good. Now he's out of my life forever.

I go back to the house, take a shower, and get to bed early. I have to be back at work in the morning. I have enough to worry about without all this drama.

I show up at the start of my shift. Caleb is working on the other truck again, so we don't see or talk to other much except when it's absolutely necessary.

We have a training session where we practice our CPR techniques, but he winds up with another partner. I get paired with Ellis again.

He's very good at doing compressions, but not so good at giving verbal cues about what he's doing and what he wants his partner to do.

He struggles to say much of anything, but he still tries. We switch back and forth for a while until the training session ends. Then Duke asks us all to give each other feedback on how our partner did.

I tell Ellis what I saw in his performance. He barely looks at me and only nods when I finish. "Now you tell me what you thought of my performance," I tell him. "What do you want to give me feedback on?"

He keeps his eyes cast down to the floor and doesn't say a word. I wait, and when he still doesn't say anything, I glance to the front of the room and make eye contact with Duke.

The rest of the crew are all talking away giving each other feedback. Duke comes over to us. "Ellis doesn't want to give me feedback," I tell him.

Duke studies Ellis for a second and then waves that away. "Never mind. I was watching you and you did fine, Allison. Why don't you pack up your mannequin and we'll get back to work?"

Ellis helps me put the mannequin away. I don't think I've ever met anyone so attentively helpful.

It's almost like he's trying to compensate for not talking by being extra useful on the crew.

I've even heard Jessie mention that he's much more energetic when it comes to helping his crewmates now than he was before John's death.

I don't know if I could ever do anything to help Ellis, but I'm starting to care about him as much as I care about the rest of the crew.

We all finish the training session and head back out to the garage. The others do some organizing around the firehouse, but after that, they stand in a circle by the rescue truck and shoot the breeze like they usually do.

Caleb is with them, so I don't feel comfortable going over there. I don't want my presence to make him uncomfortable, either. This is his firehouse more than mine.

I'm about to make myself scarce when I see Chris, Sophie, Jessie, and Emily gathering by the bulletin board.

I go over to them. "Don't tell me you're talking about the roster again."

Emily turns around to grin at me, but the sound of screeching tires interrupts us.

I glance toward the driveway and my heart stops when Clay pulls up in his car. He gets out, storms up to the garage entrance, and barges straight for the group of guys standing by the rescue truck.

They all turn around to face him. Keith, Billy, Danny, and Carter stand on the side closest to the garage door.

They have their backs to the door and they have to break apart to turn around and face Clay.

Caleb, Josh, Drew, and George stand on the other side of the circle facing the doors.

The instant Keith and Billy pull apart, Clay charges between them, breaks the circle, pulls a gun, and aims it straight at Caleb.

John Brewer's death must have made everyone extra alert to situations like this. Keith and Billy react instantaneously, dive for Clay, and grapple him by the arms to pull him away.

Keith yanks Clay's arm aside and the gun goes off. The bullet ricochets off the garage floor and skids into the empty training room.

Keith and Billy both roar in fury. The other guys surge out of position to help, but it's already too late.

Keith and Billy tackle Clay to the ground and pin him there. They're both so much bigger than he is that they subdue him easily.

The other guys surround them. Drew, George, and even Ellis all dive on top of Clay's legs to stop him from thrashing around.

Caleb goes over there, too, but there's nothing more to do. Only Clay's head sticks out from under the pile of bodies.

"You bastard!" he rages. "You son of a bitch! I asked you to help me get her back and you betrayed me by hooking up with her! You hooked up with Allison! I trusted you, you back-stabbing traitorous cocksucker!"

"I never touched her, you idiot!" Caleb bellows. "I never looked sideways at her! I told her to straighten herself out and get her life together! What the hell are you talking about?! I never hooked up with her—ever!"

Clay comes out of his hysteria just long enough to hear this. He stares up at Caleb in stunned shock and then bursts into more guttural screams.

"You lied, you bitch! You lied to me! You stabbed me in the heart and you lied!"

He erupts in wordless bellows of pain and betrayal and wrenches himself all the way over on his side. He fights Keith off just enough for Clay to bring the gun closer to his head.

Keith sees what Clay is about to do, makes another all-out dive for Clay's arm, and knocks the gun away.

Clay's wrist slams down on the floor hard enough to discharge the gun a second time. Caleb springs forward and stamps his boot on top of Clay's wrist to hold his arm down, kicks the gun away, and sends it sliding across the floor to bump into the wall.

Clay howls in pain—not just physical pain. That sound sets my hair on end. Caleb takes his foot off Clay's arm, but Clay doesn't stop.

He bursts into loud, screaming, roaring, brutal sobs. He thrashes back and forth just as hard, but he can't break the grip of five bigger, stronger men lying on top of him.

I stand across the floor watching in horror as the scene unfolds. I'm still standing there in petrified silence when the Police show up, cuff Clay, and march him still sobbing to the nearest squad car.

They lock him in and then go through the crew one person at a time taking statements from everyone. I can't move. I feel ice cold.

I don't know what to think or what to feel. I never imagined I would send Clay over the edge like this.

He tried to kill Caleb, and when Clay found out that I lied about hooking up with Caleb, Clay tried to kill himself.

This is awful. Caleb is right. I'm in no state to get involved with anyone if I could do something like this to someone I supposedly care about.

I don't recognize myself. I don't recognize my life. I have no idea who I am or what I'm doing anymore.

I'm a paramedic at Howe Firehouse. That's all I am. Everything else is completely unknown.

I'm lost. I'm adrift. I'm at sea in an ocean of uncertainty.

Chapter 14: Caleb

I push open Duke's office door and walk in. "Come on in, man," he tells me. "Shut the door and take a seat."

I shut the door and sit down in the chair across his desk, but I have a hard time looking at him.

I don't know how or where or why, but I'm the one who did this. I brought all this trouble and disaster on the firehouse.

The Police just left after spending hours interviewing everyone in the whole damn fire crew.

They went through the whole torturous process while Clay sat handcuffed and sobbing his eyes out in the back of a squad car. Poor guy.

Duke leans back in his chair and regards me across the desk. He doesn't even have to say it. We both know why I'm here.

"So....talk to me, man," he begins. "Talk me through what's going on—with you, with this guy, with Allison, with everything."

"There's nothing going on with me and Allison," I mutter under my breath. "There never has been, and if you really want to know the truth, there probably never will be."

"Then why does Clay think there is? Why does he keep bringing it up?"

"I asked her out. That's all—but that was before I knew about him. I never did or said anything after I found out about him. I swear it. They split up over the whole thing and then she asked me out, but I turned her down because she was still too in the middle of this whole thing. Her life isn't in the best place. I told her to concentrate on pulling it together and get clear of this before she thinks about going out with anyone." I look away again. "She's thinking about moving away back to wherever it is she comes from."

He studies me extra closely. I don't know if these guys go through some kind of lie detection training when they become Fire Chiefs. I really wouldn't be surprised.

Duke has the same uncanny knack for looking straight into a person. John used to do that the same way. The guy could pick up a lie like a bloodhound.

I'm not lying, though. Someone else is. "So she lied to him? Is that what you're telling me?"

I have to keep my head turned when I nod. "You weren't there. You didn't hear him. That's why he tried to shoot himself. He asked me to talk to her to try to help him get her back. I talked to her, but I didn't tell her that. I told her to get her life together. She got mad about it and told him she hooked up with me. He completely freaked out. The other guys were subduing him and he completely fell apart when he realized she lied about having a relationship with me."

"What are you going to do about that?"

"I'm not going to do anything about it. It's all over as far as I'm concerned. I don't see how anything can ever happen between me and Allison now—and I don't even want it to. I just wish I wasn't the one who brought all this chaos and all these problems into the firehouse."

"I don't see that you did, man," he tells me. "I don't see how you could have done anything differently—except the part about how you started hitting on her the minute she walked in the door."

I look away again. "Fine. Let's call it that. You were right. It was stupid of me."

"I don't call it the smartest thing you've ever done, but I don't think that on its own makes you responsible for all this chaos and problems."

"Of course it does. He never would have latched onto this idea that we did anything if I only kept my mouth shut."

"But as you said, you didn't know she was with someone. Did she tell you that before—like the minute you started hitting on her?"

"No, she never told me until after I asked her out."

"Then as far as I'm concerned, none of this is your doing. You backed off when I told you to and you dropped it completely once you did find out. He had no reason to beat you up—and there was never any reason for him to try to shoot you just now."

I look away again. I can't look at him. "Like the crew needs to go through all of this again now of all times."

"I'll be talking to Allison after this. I haven't seen anything in either of your job performances that would justify changing your work routine. You'll continue to work together on shifts. Are you cool with that?"

"Sure. She's a good paramedic."

"You two work well together. You've conducted yourself with perfect professionalism around her. I respect that. I know you'll keep doing the job the best way you know how no matter who you're working with....."

"Of course. I would never do anything else."

"That's great to hear. You can go. Thanks, Caleb. You're an asset to this crew. This will all blow over and you'll be able to get back to your regularly scheduled programming."

I can only mutter, "Not soon enough," and get out of his office.

I have a hard time making eye contact with any of my crewmates downstairs. No one has to draw me a picture about what would have happened if Clay actually shot me, too, after we just lost John. That would have been an absolute living nightmare.

Keith comes over to me and asks me if I'm okay. I don't want him or Danny comforting me.

I just feel terrible for Clay. That guy has to be hurting right now.

I stumble through the rest of my shift. I just want to take my stuff, go home, and crawl into a hole with my eyes shut for the next twelve hours before I have to function again.

The guy actually tried to kill me—and then he tried to kill himself.

I'm not on the straight and narrow like I thought I was—like I told myself I should be. I'm the one who has to pull my life together.

I admit it was childish and unprofessional of me to hit on Allison at the beginning. Duke is right about that.

Other than that, I don't see where I did wrong. She never told me to stop it. She never told me she was with Clay.

She could have shut me down right there in the firehouse driveway that first day.

She doesn't wear an engagement ring. I might have noticed if she did. Or she could have just come out and said. She didn't. Maybe Clay has a point and she did it to encourage me.

I'm just taking my duffel bag out of my locker when she comes in. I barely look at her.

She should be taking her stuff out of her locker and leaving for the day, but instead, she comes straight over to me.

"Are you okay?" she asks. "I'm really sorry about what happened."

I just say, "I'm fine," shut my locker, and walk out of the room.

She follows me out to the parking lot talking in my ear all the way there. "I'm sorry I lied to Clay about us. I had no idea he would react like that. I wouldn't have done it if I had known. I just wanted to make it all stop. I know you were right about us and I need to pull my life together...."

I stop next to my pickup and turn around to face her. I have to deal with her. I can't just walk away—much as I would like to.

"There is no us," I tell her too harshly. "Get that through your head. There is no us and there never will be."

"You mean......" She stops midsentence and her face drains of all color. "You mean....."

She freezes staring at me.

"How could you lie to him about that?" I ask. "You're supposed to care about the guy. All of this happened because you lied. Don't you get that?"

"I know!" she counters. "I just wanted to hurt him....."

My eyes pop. "You *wanted* to hurt him?! You *wanted* to hurt him?! Are you serious? How could you actually *want* to hurt someone you planned to spend the rest of your life with? How could you do something like this—to all of us? Do you know what this crew has been through in the last few months?"

"I know!" She wrings her hands and shuffles her feet. "I just wanted it all to stop! He wouldn't leave me alone! He kept talking about getting back together with me! He wouldn't listen! I just wanted to say the one thing that would make him realize it was over! I couldn't think of anything else! I didn't know he would go as far as this! You have to believe me, Caleb!"

"I don't have to do anything. Did you think at all about what would happen when you told him that? Did you think about the consequences at all—for any of us? Did you think about the consequences for him—or for me?"

She opens her mouth to argue back—but she stops herself. She shuts her mouth and looks down at the ground. "No, you're right. I didn't think about the consequences at all—for anyone. I just wanted to shut him down as quickly as possible. You're right. I should have thought it through first before I said something like that."

"You shouldn't have said it at all," I fire back. "Now the guy is on suicide watch in Howe County Jail facing a life prison sentence."

"I know," she chokes.

I turn back to my truck. "Maybe you should go see the guy and try to smooth things over."

She gasps out loud. "You can't possibly mean that!"

"I don't mean get back together with him. I mean maybe try to ease some of the damage you caused to his life. His life is over because of you. I'm not saying you're responsible for him accusing you and I'm not saying you're responsible for his actions, but he's hurting because of you. You could at least have the backbone to face him and apologize for the things you know you did wrong."

She looks down at the ground again, but her eyes always seem to come back up to meet mine.

"It's finished between us, isn't it?" she almost whispers. "There's no chance for us anymore, is there?"

"I don't see how. There are too many strikes against both of us as far as I can see."

She only nods. "I'm sorry. You're right. You deserve someone better—someone who has their shit together. Losing you......" Her voice chokes and she shakes tears out of her eyes. "If I knew then that any of this would make me lose you, that would have been consequence enough to stop me from doing it."

She stands there waiting for me to say something. Don't ask me why she's talking about losing me when she never had me.

She's right that it's over between us—all of it. I can't have a woman bringing this kind of turmoil into my life.

I would rather stay single forever than go through this. This will be a lesson to me not to hit on any woman I don't know.

I wait a minute before she says, "Bye, Caleb," and goes back inside the firehouse. Now I can go home and try to put all of this behind me.

Chapter 15: Allison

I jump again when I hear a door slam somewhere. I shiver when I look around the stark walls and impenetrable locked doors of the Howe County Jail.

This place gives me the creeps. I don't want to be here at all. I can't imagine how anyone could stay here for an indefinite period of time—maybe even decades.

Clay is facing that. He's been in here for a week already waiting for his sentencing hearing. I don't know why it's taking so long because he's already pled guilty to all the charges.

A bunch of armed guards comes into the waiting room where I stand around with a dozen other people.

Some of them are women with children. Others are men in business suits. They're probably lawyers.

The guards open another door and everyone starts filing through it into a different room. It's a long room with desks sectioned by partitions between them.

A small piece of table separates the two chairs where a prisoner and a visitor can sit. There's no protective glass or anything like that to keep the prisoner and the visitor apart.

Clay is already sitting there with his hands handcuffed in his lap. He wears orange pants and an orange shirt with a number printed on the front.

He barely looks up when I sit down opposite him.

"Hi," I tell him. "How are you?"

He shrugs without looking up.

"I just wanted to tell you I'm really sorry I lied to you about Caleb. It was a heartless, stupid thing to do and I regret it now. I regret hurting you—and I regret that I did it deliberately to hurt you. That was wrong of me. I'm sorry that things didn't work out between us. I know we both had such high hopes for moving here. I wish like anything that things could have worked out differently."

He only shrugs again. "It doesn't matter."

"It does matter!" I tell him. "You matter! I never meant to do anything that could make you try to take your own life. Is there anything I can do for you? Is there anything you need?"

"I don't need anything," he mumbles. "Just go be with him if you want to be. He's a better man than I am."

I sink back in my chair. "I won't be with him. There's no chance for that now. He won't even consider it after what I did to you."

Clay's eyes dart up. "Is that why you're here? Are you trying to get him back?"

"I can't get him back, Clay," I tell him. "I can't get him at all. That's what I'm telling you. I screwed up. I'm here because I want to somehow make up for what I did to you. This isn't about Caleb because there will never be anything between me and him. There never was and now it's all finished. We're working together. That's all."

He stares at me for a minute. I don't know what he expected from this visit.

I don't know what I expected, either. I don't hold out any hope that anything could happen between me and Caleb anymore.

Maybe, someday, if I work hard, I'll be able to straighten my life out enough to get another guy marginally as good as he is.

It won't be him. He's too good and I'm too messed up. He's right. I bring too much mayhem and trouble to his life. I'm a problem for him and I don't want to be that.

I don't want to be a problem for anyone—not even Clay.

He finally looks away. "I hope you have a good life," he mutters. "I hope things get better for you after I'm gone."

"I hope things get better for you, too," I tell him and I really mean it.

"You should go." He nods toward the door. "Don't spend any more time hanging around or worrying about me. Just concentrate on living your life and let me live mine."

"Are you sure?" I open my mouth to say something else and stop myself.

He just told me to go. Maybe hanging around here trying to make up for my mistake is actually creating a problem for him.

That must be what he means. He wants to move on with his life—whatever it's going to be. Me being here isn't helping him.

He nods toward the door again. "Go," he tells me.

I open and close my mouth a few more times before I realize what he means. Then I just stammer, "Okay.....bye....."

I want to say more. I want to tell him to take care of himself and to have a good life and all that, but he obviously doesn't want me to say any of that.

I get up and walk out of the building. Now I'm alone.

The world looks bleak and depressing when I get outside. Everything I thought I knew about my life is over.

My house is full of nothing but boxes. I'm holding an estate sale on Saturday to sell the furniture. The house sale will be finalized next week. I already have a rental apartment in town. I'll be moving in on Monday after work.

I stop on the sidewalk outside the jail. Clay is out of my life at last, but I can't even be happy about this.

Something went drastically wrong with my life if all of this could happen—not just to me but to everyone around me.

Caleb really knows so much more about these things than I do. I really need to listen to him.

I would have been much better off staying with Clay and living the rest of my life with him than for any of this to happen.

I'm a walking disaster. I have always looked down on women who bring this kind of drama and upheaval to the people around them.

Now I'm one of them. I need to make some major changes to my life—and now I'm about to.

I've already gotten hauled up in front of Chief Broebeck to explain everything that led to Clay trying to shoot Caleb in the firehouse garage.

I've never gotten hauled up in front of the Fire Chief for anything—ever. This is a new low in my career.

That on its own tells me all I need to know.

He wanted to know if I planned to stay in Howe after this. I told him that I will.

Working for the fire crew is the one and only stable thing I have in my life right now. It's the one solid anchor point that makes my life make any sense.

I need to be around strong, stable, intelligent, honorable people so I can learn from them. I need their example to show me how to live.

Caleb is that for me now. Nothing can ever happen between us, so he'll just be one of the people on the crew who offers me a model for how to live my life.

I drive back to the house and get busy organizing my uniforms, lunches, and other stuff for the week ahead.

My life is boring, routine, and uneventful now. This is the way it should be. This is the way the best people at the firehouse work.

Our jobs are stressful enough. Every call is an event and a challenge.

The rest of our lives need to be stable and routine with no surprises. That's the lesson I'm learning from all of them.

Keith. Danny. Caleb. Billy. Chris and Josh. Carter and Sophie.

They just live their lives getting through the day and raising their families in between the excitement of calls.

No one wants to deal with drama and stress in their personal lives. That would be too much to cope with. We definitely can't have anyone bringing additional drama and stress into the firehouse. No one can tolerate that.

I finish my chores, get into my pajamas, and crawl into bed with a book. That's as exciting as my life gets these days and that's the way it's going to stay.

I have a long way to go to rebuild what I lost.

The important thing for me to remember is that I know better now. I learned a massive lesson from all of this.

I took my life for granted. I never thought anything like this could happen to me. I thought I was too good for this.

I won't get into another relationship—not for a long time. I'll take Caleb's advice and just concentrate on getting through this.

It could be years before I consider dating anyone again—and that's okay. I don't want to date anyone. Having a stable, sustainable, functional life with no drama is much more important.

Chapter 16: Caleb

I look up from my lunch when the firehouse alarm goes off. The crew sits around the table in the breakroom. Then we all jump up and scramble to get out of the room fast enough.

I have to put my food back in the fridge before I run downstairs and dive into the rescue truck with the others.

Ellis, Danny, and I occupy the middle seat with Keith and Billy up front. Josh and Allison ride in the back.

"House fire on Finch Street!" Billy tells us. "No word yet on casualties!"

"Is it just one house?!" Keith calls back.

"That's all it says! House fire."

We clamber into our turnouts and go over our SCBAs again. None of us finds anything wrong with them.

Josh and Allison put on their turnouts and SCBAs, too. We unload outside the house to find the Police holding back a bunch of neighbors and other people.

Duke goes to talk to the Police. "The old lady who lives next door says the father and older kids are at school and work," the officer tells us. "The mother stays home with twin babies. The neighbor says the mother and the little ones are still inside."

Duke turns to all of us. "Let's go, folks! You should be able to get in through the kitchen in the back. Work your way forward until you find them and get out the same way. Keith, you supervise the hoses."

We split up. Josh and Allison come with Danny, Ellis, and me to the backyard. We turn on our SCBAs before we approach the kitchen door.

This side of the house isn't on fire yet. The flames cover the front of the house, the living room, and the garage.

Danny breaks into the kitchen. He has to chop his axe through the window and break out the pane so he can stick his gloved hand inside to unlock the door.

We search the kitchen and don't find anything. We search the laundry room, the bathroom, and the father's office.

The family also has another room set up as the kids' playroom with toys all over the floor. Ellis points at some half-empty baby bottles overturned on the floor.

"The mother must have just been in here when the fire started!" Danny yells through his mask. "We need to search the rest of the house. Josh, you and Ellis come with me and we'll check upstairs. Caleb and Allison—search the rest of the downstairs."

We split up and the three guys go upstairs. I point down the hall. "Let's check the living room!" I tell Allison. "It's in the front of the house closest to the fire, but the mother may have panicked and tried to get out through the front door."

She nods. Working with her is exactly the same as working with anyone else on the crew.

Three weeks have passed since the shooting at the firehouse and Clay's arrest. No one mentions the disastrous way her employment started here. Everyone would rather forget it.

She seems to want to forget it, too. No one can find any fault in the way she conducts herself on the crew. She never indicates by word, action, or even facial expression that there was ever anything between us—because there wasn't.

Her behavior gives me a profound sense of relief. We can all go back to our normal lives now. I can concentrate on keeping to the straight and narrow path without any distractions or problems.

We get to the living room, but we have to draw back when a blast of volcanic air billows through the doorway from inside. Flames consume the whole front wall of the house.

The firehose pounds against the wall and adds to the noise. We can't even get inside.

"Get down on the floor!" I yell through my mask to Allison. "You go left and I'll go right! We'll meet back here! If we can't find them, we'll pull out. Okay?"

She nods and we get down on the floor.

The fire gives the only light in the room except for one window on the other wall. I set off to crawl around the couch to the other side of the room.

I don't expect to find anything and I don't—not until I get all the way to the far corner. Two little toddlers lie unconscious on the floor. One is a boy and one is a girl.

I turn them over and check their pulses and breathing. Soot surrounds their noses and mouths and clings to the corners of their eyes. They must have smoke inhalation.

They rasp when they breathe, but at least they both are breathing. Their skin is still pink, so they're getting enough oxygen.

I cast a desperate glance around. My first thought is to take them back to the kitchen.

I look over my shoulder in that direction to decide how to tell Allison where I'm going.

When I do look, I see the fire crawling across the doorway. It swallows that part of the house. We're trapped in here.

Flames eat their way across the ceiling. We don't have much time before Allison and I will have to escape from here, even if it means leaving the patients behind.

Right then, Allison comes scuttling around the other side of the couch. "I found the mother!" She takes one look at the little ones. "How bad are they?"

"They're still breathing and their profusion looks good! Their pulses are strong and steady. They just have smoke inhalation. We need to get them out now! What's going on with the mother?"

"She's critical! I need your help, though. She's too heavy for me to carry."

"I'll get her. Where is she?"

I forget what I'm doing for a second and start to stand up. Allison grabs me and yanks me down hard. "You can't! You won't be able to carry her." Her eyes dart around the room. "That window is the only way out.....and there's a fire extinguisher by the fireplace. Get that and cover me while I put the kids out the window. Then I'll drag the mother over and you'll have to lift the mother out. Okay?"

I nod at her. I get another rush of relief that I'm here with her. She's as solid and reliable a member of our crew as I could hope for.

I set off to crawl around the couch in the other direction. I can't go near the doorway now. The fire is escalating fast.

I grab the fire extinguisher and retreat to the window. Allison has already moved the two toddlers over there. She's waiting for me.

I hand her my axe. "Get ready! As soon as you break the window, the rush of air will cause a draft."

"Got it!" she yells.

"Don't stand up until I start spraying!"

She nods back at me. Of course she knows what to do. I don't have to worry about her.

I face the fire. It rolls into the room and forms monstrous flame shapes right in front of me.

Now I understand what Carter meant when he said he has nightmares about seeing shapes in the flames. It really is true. The fire becomes a hideous, devouring monster coming after all of us.

I don't even know where the mother is. I just have to concentrate on getting these kids and Allison out of the house alive.

I pull the pin on the fire extinguisher, depress the handle, and unleash a cloud from the extinguisher at the flames.

She jumps to her feet, swings my axe at the window, and a colossal blast of scorching air hits both of us.

We both yell out as the heat sears us through our turnouts, but neither of us can stop now.

I keep spraying and back up to give her cover. The open window feeds the fire even faster.

Allison smashes out the glass as well as she can and practically tosses the two kids out the window onto the grass. She lowers them just enough to stop herself from hurting them.

"Where's the mother?!" I bellow when she comes back inside.

"She's over there by the bookshelf! Give me the extinguisher!" she roars. "You'll be able to drag her faster than I will!"

I don't want to let go of the fire extinguisher, but now isn't the time to argue. The mother must be heavy.

I hand it over and crawl across the room. The heat becomes unbearable.

Allison can't stand up anymore. She gets down on her knees and showers the flames with the fire extinguisher to protect me on our way around the couch.

I spot the mother. She is heavy. She probably weighs more than I do.

I don't dare to get off the floor. I grab her by the wrists, stretch her arms above her head, and drag her one painful inch at a time across the room.

I have to summon every ounce of my strength to heave her onto the windowsill. Then I have no choice but to flop her out the window. I don't have time to make sure I don't hurt her. At least she's alive.

I glance over my shoulder to make sure Allison is okay. She isn't. The fire extinguisher is empty and she cowers on the floor right behind me.

She holds her arms over her head against the raging heat. I don't have time to tell her to get up.

I grab her, muscle her toward the window, and heft her across the windowsill before I flip her the rest of the way out.

A punishing woof of flame hits me in the back and blows my SCBA apart just as I dive through the window.

I hit the grass with oxygen venting from my tank. I don't have the strength to get it off, but I don't have to.

The other firefighters attack me, strip off my mask, and pull my arms out of the straps. They leave the tank on the grass and four of them carry me clear of the house.

I can't move or protest while Josh tears my turnouts open and does an exam on me. I'm breathing too heavily to tell him that I'm okay. I'm just exhausted. I can't even bring myself to open my eyes.

I hear all the guys and the paramedics talking all around me. I can't understand what they're saying and I don't care. Their voices are music to my ears. I'm okay. I made it out.

Chapter 17: Caleb

I lie on the gurney in the back of the ambulance with my eyes closed when someone squeezes my shoulder.

I crack my eyes open and shut them immediately when I see Duke sitting next to me. Josh sits on the bench seat next to him.

"How are you doing, champ?" Duke asks.

"I'm taking next week off of work, boss," I husk.

He laughs. "Okay. You got it."

"I wasn't serious." I pry my eyes open. "Is everyone else okay? Is Allison okay?"

"She's fine. She says you saved her life."

I snort. "That's a good one."

"The mother and the two kids are in the hospital, but they're going to be okay, too. You saved the day again."

I look away. "Tell me I don't have to go to the hospital."

"Josh says you don't have to. He says you just need to rest. You can stay in here. We'll drive you back to the firehouse and you can go home for the rest of the day."

"I don't want to go home for the rest of the day."

"You aren't much good to us like this," Josh interjects. "Rest up and get your strength back."

I want to protest, but he's right. I can't move.

Duke stands up and squeezes my shoulder again. "Take all the time you need. You earned it."

He steps out of the ambulance and disappears around the other side of the vehicle. Josh keeps writing on his clipboard to finish his paperwork.

I wilt onto the gurney. I can see through the open ambulance doors that the rest of the crew is still out there working.

Keith and the others move around the house spraying down the flames. I don't see the other ambulance. The paramedics are still here helping out the guys wherever possible.

Allison crosses the yard on her way somewhere else. She looks fine. She isn't lying flat on her back in an ambulance.

She didn't have to lift that mother through the window. I still find it hard to believe I was even able to get her off the floor.

I let my eyes sink shut, and a minute later, Josh takes my blood pressure again. I keep my eyes shut for that.

He also sticks his stethoscope down my shirt to listen to my lung sounds and presses his fingers to my wrist to check my pulse.

I can't resent him for handling me like this. I'm his patient. He's responsible for making sure I'm okay and I stay that way.

I'm still lying there like an enormous slug when he buckles the safety straps around me, slams the back doors shut, buckles himself in, and the ambulance drives away down the street.

We drive back to the firehouse and George backs the unit into the garage. That's it. I can't stay lying down anymore.

I still don't want to take the day off of work, but I can't stay here.

I wait until Josh unbuckles me. Then I haul my flabby carcass out of the back. I have to sit down to take my turnouts off.

I'm putting my pants and boots into the rescue truck when Danny shows up with my jacket and helmet. "We're sending your SCBA in for maintenance. You need to set up a new apparatus."

I nod and turn away. Everything I do costs me a massive effort.

I take myself off to the oxygen tank cage and fit the new tank with a regulator, pressure valve, and a new mask.

I go over everything in minute detail. I don't want anything going wrong with the apparatus when I need it.

The rest of the crew is already upstairs in the breakroom when I put the new apparatus in the rescue truck to replace the old one.

I'm alone in the garage, so I sink onto the truck step and draw in a shaky breath. I'm sitting there when Allison comes over to me. "You okay?" she asks. "Josh said you were really wrung out."

"Duke told me to take the rest of the day off. I don't want to, but now I'm thinking he's right. I don't think I can handle climbing the stairs, much less face another call."

She peers at me extra closely. "Thank you—for what you did for me. I owe you."

"Forget it," I mutter. "I was just doing my job."

"That's what I mean. You're always just doing your job when you save people. You did it for Clay and you did it for me." She leans forward, places her hand on my shoulder, and squeezes. "You're a prince, Caleb. It really is a privilege to work with you."

She takes her hand away immediately and walks away toward the stairs.

That touch doesn't mean anything more than when Duke does it, but her hand feels different. I can't remember her ever touching me before—except when we accidentally bumped into each other during calls.

I barely noticed when I touched her to pick her up earlier. I actually had my arms around her body and held her against me, but I hardly felt it at all.

Now all those moments come rushing back to me. Her hand feels so different on my shoulder than Duke's does—and not because her hand is smaller and weaker.

Having her squeeze my shoulder means so much more. It isn't just a comradely token of affection. I know she means it as one, but her touch brings with it so many other hidden suggestions.

I don't know what to think or what to feel. I respect her too much and I care too much about our working relationship ever to take it further, but it sure does bring up a lot of hidden feelings.

I'm still sitting there when Duke comes back. He drives his support pickup around the back of the firehouse and then walks into the garage.

He cocks his head when he sees me sitting there. "You okay?"

"I'm going to take the rest of the day off after all."

"Good," he replies. "Take two or three if you have to."

"Let's hope it doesn't come to that."

I drag myself to the locker room, get my stuff, and head out to my truck. I drive home, go straight to my bedroom, and collapse.

I take a few minutes to change out of my uniform and get into my pajamas. That's all I can handle today.

I get into bed, bury my face under the covers, and shut my eyes, but this haze of exhausted sleep sweeping over me only brings up forgotten fantasies I used to have about Allison.

I'll never act on them, but they excite my body more than ever, now that I'm not wearing my uniform. Maybe I'm already dreaming so I'm not thinking clearly.

I drift off thinking about her curves.....and what she looked like in that red dress at the bar.....and the way her breasts bulged through her tight T-shirt that first day I met her.

I feel myself starting to get hard thinking about her and I immediately push those thoughts away. I'm not going there—not after I finally worked myself and her into a situation where we can work together in harmony with no dramas.

Chapter 18:
Allison

I stand at attention with the rest of the fire crew and listen to the Mayor of Howe give a speech about all the selfless men and women who dedicate their lives and put their necks on the line to save lives every day.

He's only the first of many to give speeches today. We all wear our dress uniforms and the Police force turns out in full dress uniform to stand next to us.

I recognize a lot of people in the crowd listening, including the family from the burning house.

The Mayor finishes talking and then Police Chief Jim Walker stands up. He gives another, almost identical speech before he goes through the assembled Police officers and honors a bunch of people with decorations for valor and heroism.

Chief Walker tells the story of each person's actions and the crowd applauds when the person goes up there to receive their decoration.

They all smile and blush with pride when they take their places on the platform. A bunch of families yell extra loudly when their loved ones get decorated.

Some kids in the crowd wave signs saying, *Best Dad Ever,* and *My Dad is a Hero.*

Some of the Police officers wave back at their families before they come back to attention.

The crowd goes wild when Chief Walker announces that these are all the decorations he's handing out today and encourages everyone to give the Police heroes a round of applause.

Everyone is smiling, but I can't. I'm getting decorated along with Billy, Carter, Ellis, and Caleb, but I can't get excited about it.

I'm starting to understand what Caleb means. I was just doing my job by saving those people. I don't want any special recognition for it.

In a way, getting decorated is just a distraction from the task of keep my life on track. Anything else is just extra and doesn't really mean anything.

It's a temptation to think I'm something more important than I am.

Duke gets up on the platform next and gives another glowing speech about the outstanding work the fire crew does every day to keep this town safe. A lot more people applaud. I don't let myself turn around to see who is cheering for us this time.

Duke starts off by telling a story about Billy saving a family from a burning house and then saving the same family when their deranged father tried to run them over with his car. Billy threw himself on top of one of the kids, saved his life, and Billy got hit instead.

I didn't know that story until today. No one ever talks about it. Then again, no one on the fire crew ever talks about their past saves.

That call must have meant a lot to Billy because he has tears in his eyes when he goes up to the platform to get decorated for his bravery.

A different family I don't know bursts into cheers from the other side of the crowd. The kids yell Billy's name and he struggles to smile and wave at them when he turns around to stand at attention next to the podium.

Then Duke tells the story about Carter pulling two teenagers from a burning shed at the elementary school. A hush falls over the crowd when everyone sees what he looks like, but he doesn't bat an eyelash.

He stands at attention while Duke tells another story about Carter pulling an injured, unconscious fellow firefighter out of a burning house.

Duke doesn't mention that the injured firefighter was Andy Skinner, the man who shot John Brewer and tried to kill Carter.

Carter shows no emotion when he gets decorated a second time. The crowd doesn't cheer as wildly. Too many people in this town already know the whole story.

Then Duke tells the story about Ellis saving Carter's life from the lunatic gunman who killed John Brewer. Ellis doesn't smile or even raise his eyes.

He lurches through the process of getting decorated and standing in line with us. Only faint applause greets him when he comes to attention. John Brewer's death casts a long shadow over this town.

Duke goes on to tell about Caleb and me saving that family. Duke decorates us and we stand at attention in line with the others.

Then I stay where I am while Duke tells the story and decorates Caleb a second time for saving not just Clay but the other three families from the car crash.

All of this happens at a distance from me. I'm much prouder of my crewmates than I am of myself. These people standing around me are the real heroes.

I was just doing my job. I didn't do anything special even if Duke says I did.

I know the rest of the crew feels the same way. That's what makes them true heroes, but I don't see myself that way.

We have a big reception after the ceremony. Everyone congratulates us, shakes hands, and hugs us. We stand around eating, but I can't enjoy that, either.

I'm on a strict nutrition plan these days to improve my fitness. I want to get stronger so I'll be able to do my job better. Indulging in a bunch of cake and junk food snacks isn't as important as it used to be.

The mother Caleb and I saved from the house comes over with her little ones, her husband, and her two older children.

She hugs me and Caleb with tears in her eyes and then the rest of the family does the same thing.

I find myself cringing when I hug her. I don't want to let myself go the way she obviously has.

I wouldn't want any firefighter to struggle to pick me up if he had to rescue me from a burning house. There never was a cake made that tastes good enough for that.

The reception ends and the on-duty fire crews and Police officers go back to work. The civilian guests and well-wishers keep standing around talking.

I slip away. I have the day off and I don't want to spend it here.

I go home, change out of my uniform, do a workout, clean my house, make some extra food for the coming week, and put all my affairs in order.

I have tomorrow off, too, but I don't want to slouch around the house wasting my life.

I put on my casual jeans and a long-sleeved button-up shirt, drive out of town to the mountains outside of Howe, find a hiking trail on the map, and set off through the trees.

It's so peaceful here. I can forget about everything, including the fact that I just got decorated for heroism.

I climb to the top of a peak, follow the trail over a few different saddles and passes, and come to another even higher hilltop. It looks out westward—away from Howe.

I can't see any sign of humanity from up here. Rolling wilderness spreads out before me as far as the eye can see.

I'm a paramedic with the Howe County Fire Department. I've worked hard these last three weeks to erase every other aspect of my identity. I don't want any other identity.

That part of who I am makes sense. I don't have to figure out any of the rest of it. I want to get lost in it.

I sit there for a long time—hours, maybe. I don't have to be anywhere in particular.

I didn't bring any camping equipment—or any food or water. The sun starts to sink toward the western horizon. I'll have to go back to town before dark, but I don't want to leave.

I don't want to go back to any life that requires me to be something more than this. I just want to sit here in the silence and feel that the rest of my life no longer exists.

I'm a paramedic. No one needs to know anything else about me and I don't need to know anything else about me.

The wind blows through my hair. It gets colder and I don't have a jacket to keep me warm. I should stand up and leave, but I decide to wait just a little longer to watch the sun set. Then I'll go.

Just then, I hear footsteps on the path behind me. I glance in that direction thinking it will be some other hikers.

I freeze when Caleb comes out of the trees.

He stops in his tracks and regards me from a distance. He's wearing casual hiking clothes, too.

He looks like he's been working out a lot lately. He looks like he put on a few more inches of muscle since I first met him.

His face is leaner and more serious. He doesn't joke around the way he used to. I mean, he still jokes around with the rest of the crew, but he doesn't get as silly or suggestive as he once did.

His whole personality seems to have gotten a lot more serious after the whole Clay disaster. I can't imagine Caleb hitting on a girl the way he hit on me. He learned a lesson there.

I expect him to leave when he sees me there, but instead, he comes over to me and sits down next to me. "Hi," he murmurs.

"Hi," I reply. "Congratulations on today."

"You, too." He keeps his voice low and stares out at the sunset. "You deserve it after the way you acted in that house."

"You deserve it, too. I couldn't have done it without you."

He doesn't look at me. "I know we say this all the time now, but I really value you as a member of our crew."

I look away. "I still have a long way to go to make up for the things I did."

He glances at me once. "Are you okay about it all?"

"Oh, sure. I'm fine. Just trying to stay on the straight and narrow, you know."

He stares at me extra closely. For someone who wouldn't look at me at all a second ago, he sure is drilling me with an intense stare now.

Maybe I said the wrong thing. Maybe he doesn't understand what I mean about the straight and narrow.

He finally tears his gaze away and goes back to watching the sunset. The air is getting colder and I shiver. The sky turns pastel colors and the sun lights up the clouds with a rim of gold.

"Have you heard from Clay?" he asks.

"Not since the shooting. I went to see him the way you suggested. I talked to him like you said and apologized—for everything. That was the last time I saw him."

"I suppose he's long gone by now," Caleb murmurs. "He'll be in prison for a long time."

"No, he isn't in prison yet. He's still in Howe County Jail."

His head shoots up. "He is? Why? It's been almost a month. The Department of Corrections should have sent him upstate before now."

"There were some problems with his plea deal. The Police offered him a deal based on the charges, but the District Attorney rescinded it when the lab reports came back on the shooting. I didn't look into the details, but the DA had to issue another plea deal and then Clay had to negotiate it with his lawyer before they accepted it. They had to have another plea hearing before Clay got sentenced. The whole thing delayed the process and Clay was still on suicide watch for a while afterward. Both his lawyer and the DA went back and forth a few times trying to decide if they should go for some kind of insanity defense."

Caleb won't stop staring at me. "So what happened?"

"He got sentenced under the original charges. He didn't use an insanity defense, but he had to undergo some psych evaluations before they sent him upstate. He's still at Howe. I don't know how long they'll keep him here, but this all counts toward his sentence. They'll take the time he spends at Howe off the full sentence. It doesn't really matter whether he does the time here or upstate."

Caleb finally looks away. "Wow. Remind me never to let anything like that happen to me."

"It couldn't happen to you. You're way too good for that. I, on the other hand, already did let it happen to me. I have as much to make up for as he does."

He doesn't answer nor does he look at me. He definitely doesn't contradict. Maybe he understands better than he lets on how much I really contributed to the whole situation.

I got myself into that mess. No one did that for me. I can't claim that Clay did it all. I didn't keep the reins on my life and it all blew up in my face.

"How are you doing with it all?" I ask and then a sudden thought makes me stiffen. "You haven't seen Clay, have you?"

"No, I haven't, but I would have if I had known he was in Howe. I would have visited him before now. I owe him an apology. I'll go see him now that I know he's still here."

"What do you have to apologize for? You didn't do anything. You're the injured party here."

He glances at me. "I did do something. I hit on you way too hard and way too fast. I shouldn't have done that. None of this would have happened if I kept my pants zipped."

I try to laugh at him. "You did keep them zipped. You just talked a big game."

"That's what I mean. That was all wrong and very unprofessional of me." He turns around and looks at me. "I'm sorry. None of it would have happened if I only stayed in line."

"You didn't do anything wrong as far as I'm concerned. You gave me a lot of compliments and then you asked me out. You never made my work life uncomfortable. You always did it as a perfect gentleman. You backed off immediately when you found out about Clay. I couldn't ask for better than that. I'm the one to blame if anyone is. I should have told you that very first day—the very first time you flirted with me. Then none of it would have happened."

He looks away again. "You're a lot more forgiving than I would be."

"I doubt that. Here you are blaming yourself instead of me when I'm the one who really did cause the problem. You would blame yourself even if our positions were reversed. I know you better than that."

Chapter 19: Allison

The sun sinks behind the horizon.

"It's getting too cold up here for me," I tell Caleb. "I'm going to go back to town before it gets dark. You should come, too. It will be too dark for you to find your way down the mountain pretty soon."

I stand up and so does he. We both brush the dirt off our clothes.

I turn away toward the path, but before I can leave, he catches me to stop me.

My nerves stand on end when he takes hold of my hand and pulls me back toward him. A shiver runs up my spine when his dark eyes lock on me and don't look away.

He's looking at me like that.

He laughed, joked, flirted, and teased when we first met. He never looked at me like this. He never drilled me with eyes smoldering with dark fire.

He pulls me closer by the hand and then, like magic, the fingers of his other hand glide into my hair to pull me in and kiss me.

His lips start off feather-light and so, so gentle. He kisses softly, romantically. He's always careful and polite. He kisses carefully and politely, too.

I melt into that kiss. His lips feel velvety soft and dreamy, but strong and comforting at the same time.

His hand radiates warmth up my arm, but in a second, his other hand changes the tempo to something very different.

His fingers grip tighter into my hair and his lips play a little more firmly on my mouth. They command me to respond as he kisses me harder and deeper.

His hand on the back of my head steers me against his mouth and both of our mouths open at the same time. Our tongues meet and set both of us on fire.

I collapse into that powerful hold on the back of my neck as he kisses me in full passionate energy. His mouth never stops moving back and forth, tasting, exploring, dancing around his tongue, and consuming me in so much heat. I can't think when he kisses me like this.

His body stiffens and his muscles strain to hold himself back from doing more. I want to touch him, but when I raise my hands, I only wind up touching his arms.

His shoulders and biceps swell under his jacket. His hands feel muscular and strong in my hair.

Right then, just because I'm thinking about his hands, he lets go of mine and wraps his arm behind my back.

He pulls me all the way against him while we kiss. I throw my arms around his neck and let myself fall into the bliss of finally kissing him.

So much time and trouble has passed. I never let myself think I could ever kiss him like this, but I am.

He's real. He's here. He's standing right in front of me with his arms around me.

The energy and desire between us keeps escalating. I could stand here kissing him forever. I just want to feel my arms around him and know that this is real.

He must want this. He must think it's time. He wouldn't do it otherwise.

Just then, another gust of cold air blows over the mountain peaks. His bulk warms me and his jacket protects him from the coming night, but he pulls away.

He puts me down, gives me one more light kiss, and we both set off down the path down the mountain.

The shadows get much darker as soon as we drop down the other side of the peak. We pass through dense forest where we can barely see well enough to follow the path.

Neither of us says a word while Caleb follows me all the way down to the bottom. I expect him to follow me to the parking lot where we'll both drive off in different directions.

I'm in front of him leading the way when we come to a tree fallen over the path. I stop to climb over it, but he grabs my hand again to stop me.

He moves close to me in the dark and murmurs down into my face in a breathless whisper. "Stay here and spend the night with me," he breathes. "I have a campsite near here. Come stay with me tonight."

My heart stops. We just kissed for the first time and now he's asking me to spend the night with him.

I already know what kind of a man he is. I've been working with him for weeks. I know him a lot better than I knew Clay and I was ready to marry Clay.

Caleb leans in and kisses me again—deeper this time. He pushes me back against the fallen tree and crushes me under his weight.

He doesn't try to stop me from feeling how hard he is—or how strained his breathing is getting.

He attacks my mouth, but he doesn't touch my body. He grabs the tree bark to pull himself tight against me. He undulates his body up and down me so I can feel every inch of his granite physique.

He keeps his eyes open and bores into my mind while he does it. He watches every shade of my reaction to his obvious suggestion. He isn't asking me to come back to his camp so we can talk.

Just to confirm it, he eases back just enough to break the contact of our lips. He jams his forehead into mine and pants into my mouth from inches away.

"I've wanted you so bad since I first laid eyes on you," he whispers. "I can't stop thinking about you. I dream about you at night. I want your hands on me. I want to feel your body under me. I can't take it anymore."

"I want you!" My voice breaks in a high, strained rasp. "I need you so much!"

"Come back to my tent," he whispers. "I need you with me tonight."

He stands up to let me climb over the tree, but as soon as I turn around, he attacks me again.

He throws his weight against me from behind and crushes me into the tree so I have to bend over it.

In a split second, he grabs me, wraps his arms around me, plunges one hand between my legs to rub my burning slit, and his other hand scraps up to my breasts.

He crushes my breast once and then flattens his hand on my sternum to hold me in place.

I yelp when he teases my clit through my jeans. His rock-hard package digs into my ass from behind.

He grinds me down on it while his hand teases me to oblivion. I gasp in torrential pleasure and then moan out loud. We're in the woods in the middle of the night. No one can see or hear us.

My moans rise to full cries. I'm going to climax if he doesn't stop, but just then, He takes a step forward, leans over, and flattens me against the tree lying face down.

His body pumps into me from behind, but he doesn't take his pants off—or mine. He doesn't try to take our clothes off at all.

I want him to. I want him to strip down my jeans and take me right here on this fallen tree. I want him to own me and use my body any way he wants, even if it's just a momentary passing encounter to satisfy his desire.

He sinks his mouth into my shoulder and bites me through my shirt. He grunts in animal madness while he pumps into me from behind.

His hands keep exploring every part of me, squeezing my breasts, grabbing my hips to pull me back against him, and rubbing up my back to hold me down.

I get lost in all those burning hot suggestions of all the things he's going to do to me. I want them now. I want him to take me now.

He doesn't. He eventually stands up, pulls me to my feet, and turns me around to face him.

I think he's going to kiss me again, but instead, he takes my hand and steers it between his legs.

My fingers close on his throbbing package and he lets out a very faint little gasp of pleasure through his nose when I squeeze it.

I massage him harder, follow the length of his shaft, and stroke him through his jeans. He groans each time I do it. I love that sound. I love turning him on like this.

He bows his head and shuts his eyes. I don't stop and his noises become even more strained and short as he struggles to contain himself.

He doesn't seem to notice when I kiss him on the forehead. So much affection and care pours out of me when I see him like this.

I'm just making up my mind to go down on my knees and take him in my mouth right here, but right then, he opens his eyes and pulls my hand away.

He takes it in his as though he never got me to touch him like that. He leads me away, back up the path in the direction we just came.

I don't know where he's taking me. It doesn't seem to matter. I already know what's going to happen.

Chapter 20: Caleb

I have to control my heart rate when I turn off onto the side path leading to my campsite. I'm holding Allison's hand. I kissed her .....and touched her.....and she touched me.

Nothing will ever be the same between us, but I don't want it to be the same between us. I'm done playing it safe.

I behaved myself for weeks and so did she. She proved she can walk the line if she needs to. She completely disconnected herself from Clay. She isn't tangled up in that anymore.

I lead her back to my tent and stop in front of it. It's completely dark now with the moon shining down through dappled treetops overhead.

The dim light casts a silver sheen over the tent. It's barely big enough for two people, but it will work for what we need to use it for.

I turn to face her. My package aches from her touching me like that. I could have exploded in her hand.

She looks angelic in this light. Her eyes shine with so much understanding and desire.

I've always wanted to see her like this—so receptive. She never looks away from me even once.

I want to kiss her again. I want to tear her clothes off right now and bend her over right here in the moonlight.

I also want to go slow with her. I want to make this last all night long and a whole lot longer.

In a way, how much I want her stops me from taking her at all. I just want to bathe in the knowledge that I can.

I've longed for her for so many tortured lonely nights. Now she's here and she's willing. I want to take my time and decide what to do next.

My shaft spasms in my shorts just from standing this close to her. I want her to touch me like that again. I want to erupt in her hand while we kiss for the ages.

I slip my hand into hers to take her inside the tent, but she reads my mind. Before I can move, she sinks onto her knees in front of me and nuzzles her face into my crotch.

She opens her mouth wide and closes it very gently around my package. She gazes up at me in such hungry passion....and then her eyes sink closed in ecstasy when she closes her mouth.

She does it a little harder.....a little faster.....enough to make me pant and gasp in ragged torment. She is not doing this. She is not about to suck me right here.

Her hands rise to my hips to bring me deeper into her face—and then she grabs my belt to pull open my fly.

"No, baby!" I whisper and pull her hands away. "Don't."

She stares up at me out of the mists of time. "Please...." she whispers back. "I want to. I want you in my mouth....." She tries to move her face toward me.

I pull her away by her hands. This position drives me out of my mind. My shaft pulsates trying to get into her mouth.

I can't stand to hear her begging me for it. I would love to hold her arms out to both sides while I bury my meat in her hot, ravenous mouth.

"Please...." she husks again. "Please....I need you....."

"No, baby," I whisper again. "Not yet. Later."

Her features spasm in a grimace of pure sexual abandon. She really wants it.

I hold her hands away so I can control how close I get to her.

My prick hurts from wanting her so bad. I want to be in her mouth feeling her tongue and lips exciting my shaft. I want to unload in her mouth while I control her hands and head for my pleasure.

I can't do that with her now—not on our very first night. My first act with her can't be something so rough and carnal and demeaning. She might enjoy that, but it will have to wait.

I hold her there anyway just so I can see the way she's looking up at me. My guts twist when I see that she really does want it. She wants to pleasure me in her mouth.

She would let me take her like that. She would let me bend her over a fallen tree trunk. She would let me use her mouth while I restrain her hands in the air.

She wants me to take her like that, but that isn't what I want from her—not like that—not now.

"Stand up, baby," I whisper.

She does it. I let go of her hands and she pushes herself to her feet.

I turn away, unzip the tent, and climb inside before she follows.

I sit down on my sleeping bag and then recline on my elbow while she sits down next to me on the insulated mat covering the floor.

She doesn't mention being uncomfortable. She must be cold, though.

The moonlight coming through the tent walls diffuses enough for us to see each other. I sit up, rummage in my supplies, and set up my little camping stove.

I pour water into my cooking pot, heat it up, and make her a mug of hot chocolate. I put it into her hands and she blows on it.

I dig around in my food bag and bring out a packet of cookies and a bag of trail mix. She's busy sipping her hot chocolate.

"Thank you," she breathes. "This is amazing."

"Eat something." I rip open the cookies in front of her.

She eats them and helps herself to the trail mix when I pour it into a bowl for her. She keeps looking up at me with wide eyes glassy with wonder and anticipation.

I should probably say something to lighten the mood, but I don't feel like it. This moment doesn't need to be lightened.

We're about to do something serious—something that could affect the rest of our lives. I don't want to mess it up by turning it into a joke.

I take a few cookies for myself and lean back on my elbow on my sleeping bag. She stays sitting up while she takes a few more sips of her drink.

"Did you come out here right after the ceremony?" she asks.

"Yeah, I didn't want to stay in town. I needed to think about things. This is the first time I've gotten decorated for anything. Danny is the one who usually gets decorated. I guess I had to reevaluate my whole idea of myself if I could be good enough to get decorated, too."

She stares at me. "I would have thought you would be getting decorated all the time."

"Naw. I've always been something like everybody's kid brother who is always screwing up and the older guys have to constantly straighten me out. I used to think I would be lucky if I ever got to be as good as Danny. I never had a prayer of being as good as John and Keith. Now

I have two decorations and we have a bunch of new guys on the crew. It's almost like I'm equal to them now."

She blinks at me in surprise. "You are equal to them! Even you must see that."

I shrug. "Not really. Guys like John, Duke, and Keith are in a class by themselves—and then there's Carter. That guy.....I don't even know what the hell he is."

"He seems so nice!"

"He is. He's incredibly nice. He's just a beast, you know? He's strong, tough, brave, dedicated—he's everything John, Duke, and Keith are. Carter could probably have gotten himself appointed as Fire Chief in John's place. I really wouldn't have been surprised. He probably would have had a much easier time than Duke did. We all respect Carter. You can't help but respect the guy."

She munches her cookie and swirls her hot chocolate in her mug. "I know what you mean. He's like some kind of god or something even though he looks so terrible."

"You think he looks terrible? I think he looks amazing. His scars make him look hypnotizing. I'm not surprised Sophie fell for him. He's the total package in ways no one else on the crew is."

She doesn't answer. She stares down into her mug.

I didn't bring her here to talk about Carter—or anything else. I know I should talk to her about something—maybe about what we're actually doing here together, but I already know that.

"What about you?" I ask. "Have you been decorated before?"

She keeps her head down and mumbles into her drink. "A few times—not that it means anything."

"What do you mean? How can it not mean anything?"

"I'm not sure. I guess my head has been going to some pretty strange places lately. I keep thinking nothing that happened before all of this means anything. I used to think I was pretty great. I thought I had it all—like maybe I was the total package the way you say Carter is. Now I realize how messed up I must be if I let this happen."

"You didn't let it happen."

She makes a face at me. "Of course I did. I did all of this. I did it to you. I did it to Clay and I did it to myself. When Clay got arrested for beating you up at the bar, the bail bondsman met me at the jail just before Clay was about to be released. The bail bondsman told me, 'You know, you might want to take steps to make sure this never happens again.' And he was dead right. None of this would have happened if I hadn't let it. Now I have to clean up the mess I made of my life. I have to do more than clean it up. I have to clean up the mess my life w as *before* this happened. I didn't even realize my life was a mess, but it must have been if I got myself into this—and even made it happen through my actions. I might not have meant to, but that's almost worse than if I made it happen deliberately. It's a crime of negligence. I thought I was too good to guard myself against that. I didn't think I had to because I thought I was better than people who let things like this happen. I can't let that happen again. I have to stay on track and concentrate on what's important—which is toeing the line and trying to be a good person instead of thinking I'm too good ever to make a mistake."

I don't know what to say because I see her point. I don't want to come out and say I agree with her about it being her fault, but it is. She's right about that.

She sure turned her life around. She doesn't have to be here. She never expected to be here with me.

She would have continued right on the straight and narrow way, doing the right thing, and trying to be a good person.

She is a good person. She's a good person because she realizes she messed up. Now she's trying to fix it or at least make sure it never happens again.

The change in her these last few weeks has made her so much more appealing. I could see how she was when she first walked into the firehouse driveway. She thought she was great because she was.

Maybe all of that greatness went to her head. She never thought it could all go wrong so she didn't take steps to make sure it didn't.

I can respect that. We all make mistakes and we all have to start over from nothing when we do.

She finishes her drink and puts the half-empty cookie package and the bag of trail mix back on the other side of the tent where she saw me get them out.

She brushes the cookie crumbs off her hands and lap and then leans back to stretch out on the insulated mat.

She lies down on her back and turns her head to stare straight up at me.

Chapter 21:
Allison

I stare up at Caleb. The dim light shining through the tent walls glows around him and gives me a haunted view of his features.

He stares back at me in the depths of that serious, fiery intent of his. He doesn't joke even once.

His presence radiates so much power and determination. We both know why I'm here. I'm in his tent. It's the middle of the night and we're in the middle of nowhere.

No one will ever find out what we did here. This moment is just between us.

I can let all my reservations go. I don't have to behave or do the right thing. I don't have to wonder if I might be making the biggest mistake of my life.

Caleb could never be a mistake. He's been holding me off ever since Clay broke up with me.

If Caleb thinks I'm ready, I must be. I can't think of any guy I would rather get together with. He's everything I want and he keeps his life together a hell of a lot better than I do.

If he thinks this is right, then I trust him. He wouldn't do it if he didn't think that I changed enough.

He stays propped on his elbow above me and raises his hand to touch my face. He brushes my hair out of my eyes, strokes my cheek, and then slides down to my neck.

My breath stops when he keeps going down to my shirt. He doesn't break eye contact when he starts very slowly, deliberately, and suggestively unbuttoning one button after another.

My body stretches to the breaking point when I realize he's about to undress me. His hands leave a trail of fire down my chest as he unfastens each button one after another.

"Tell me you want this," he whispers.

"Yes!" I choke. "Please....I need you....."

Saying those words costs me everything I have. He reduces me almost to tears with all this emotion welling up in me.

It breaks my heart that I could ever do anything to make myself not deserve him.

The same avalanche of emotion rushes to my crotch. My flesh aches for him. He turns me on so much....and I really do need him. I need him in every way. I need his heart and soul—not just his body.

He pushes my shirt aside and exposes my chest, stomach, and bra. The cold air chills me, but it only makes me tremble for him more.

I keep my arms down at my sides and struggle to breathe as he drags his electric fingertips across my chest, down my stomach, and then does the same with his hot, rough palm.

"Touch me...." I croak. "Please...."

"Mmmmm," he breathes. "Show me how much you want it."

I can only writhe in front of him and stare back up at him in rabid hunger as he teases my skin to the breaking point. I want him to touch my breasts, my slit—every part of me.

I want him on top of me and behind me. I want him inside me. I want to feel him taking me and owning me. I want everything he can give me and more.

"You want me, don't you, baby?" he whispers.

"Yes, Caleb!" I lose control of my voice and almost scream his name. He's killing me right now. "Please.....Don't you know how much I need you.....?"

He doesn't answer this time. He pushes my shirt a little farther back and leaves me lying there exposed while he drags his hand down between my legs.

He grabs me and starts massaging me through my jeans the way he did outside. "Show me," he tells me. "Show me how much you need me. Show me how much you want me here."

I moan, and as soon as I do, my passion for him takes over. I try to buck against his hand, but some invisible force holds me down on the ground.

I sense that he has to do this to me. I need him to be the one to do it to me. I want him to be the one to do it to me.

My arms remain pinned to the ground even though no one is holding me there. I thrash and convulse as the waves of pleasure rise and build to the breaking point.

"Beg me for it." His voice cuts deeper now in an unmistakable command. "Beg me to give it to you."

Those words spike me off the charts. I can't keep quiet anymore. I can barely hold eye contact.

"Please!" I scream. "Please....Caleb....."

Just saying those words rocket me into a reeling climax and I burst into loud screams. I can't stop myself.

I roll my head toward him trying to bury myself in him, but he holds himself at a distance.

He rubs me harder all the way through it to wring the last drops of pleasure from me. He's taking me there and he hasn't even touched me or taken my clothes off.

He eases off a little bit at a time while I wind down from the punishing waves of energy sweeping through me.

I collapse moaning and sobbing in front of him. I want to curl up in a ball and disappear in a drugged haze, but he won't let me.

"Look at me, baby," he tells me.

I drag my eyes open and almost start crying when I see the way he's looking at me. He's so magnetically handsome like this. He isn't casual or carefree or fun-loving or whatever everyone at the firehouse thinks he is.

He's powerful and dominating. I have no choice but to crumble in whimpering moans in front of him.

"Please.....kiss me....." I choke. "I need you."

He bends in and kisses me only once—very quickly. Then he pulls away, straightens up on his elbow, and goes back to running his big, strong palm up and down my chest and stomach.

He occasionally grips my breasts, but he only does it once each time and never long enough to excite me. Then he moves on.

This casual touch calms me down more than anything else he could do. My body fizzes with so much energy, but at least I can lie calmly now.

I bask in the glow of his touch and the hazy intoxication of the orgasm he just gave me. I don't want to be anywhere else. I don't want to demand that he do anything more with me.

I'm his to do what he wants with. Whatever he wants to do or plans to do with me, I make up my mind to go along with it. I won't ask for anything more.

I just want to be good enough for him. I want him to think I'm good enough for him to touch me like this.

My eyes float back open out of a distant dream when he starts unbuttoning my jeans. I stare up at him in rapture. Is he really going to take it further?

I want to say so many things to him. I want to tell him how much I want him—how much I admire him and even worship him.

All this passion makes me worship him. He looks magnificent lying there above me on his elbow.

He looks like the most perfect man I've ever seen. I know on the inside he's the most perfect man I've ever met.

I hope he can take some pleasure in me—just a small fraction of what he's giving me.

He unbuttons my jeans, unzips the zipper, and pulls them aside to reveal the top of my panties. His eyes dart down to them and then his hand migrates back up to my shirt.

He tugs at the open sides. "Take this off," he tells me.

I stay lying down while I pull my shirt off. I have to raise my shoulders to slide the shirt out from underneath me.

He takes it from me and puts it away on the other side of the tent. When he comes back, he goes back to stroking my arms and shoulders and sides this time.

I lie in front of him staring up into his hypnotic eyes. I love the way he's taking ownership of me. I love the way he undresses me with his eyes and tells me exactly what he wants.

Without warning, he sits up, takes hold of my jeans, and scoots them down to my feet. I try to help him by raising my hips. He leaves my panties in place—and I'm still wearing my bra.

He pulls off my shoes and socks and lays them and my jeans in a pile with my shirt. He puts everything on the other side of his sleeping bag where I can't get to it.

Is that his way of keeping me here overnight—as if I would suddenly change my mind and run off into the night to get away from him?

He leans back on his elbow and turns to face me like me lying here half naked in front of him doesn't mean anything to him.

He can take all the time in the world that he wants to pass his warm hands up and down my body.

He starts with my arms, chest, and stomach again.....and slowly, very slowly, each pass migrates lower to the top of my panties......and around to my hips.....and down to my thighs.

He doesn't have to tell me I'm beautiful. I know guys find me attractive, but his silence somehow means so much more.

I tremble in front of him when he touches me. My heart explodes from the way I feel when I look at him.

Some part of me understands that none of this would have been possible when we first met. He wouldn't have touched me like this and I wouldn't have responded to him like this, either.

He eventually decides it's time to slide his hands between my thighs. He glides higher toward my saturated panties, but he doesn't go that far.

"Does this excite you?" he whispers.

"Yes!" I croak.

"Do you want me to touch you here?"

"Yes!!" I break down in wretched sobs right in front of him. "Please, Caleb! Please touch me!"

"You wanted to suck me outside, didn't you?" he asks.

"Yes!" I break down whimpering and moaning again. I can't lie still.

"You wanted to feel me in your mouth, didn't you?"

I can only moan in agony when his fingers barely graze my panties between my legs.

Without warning, he takes his hand away and leans back. "Do it now."

It takes me way too long to pull my brain back into some kind of functioning state. I struggle to sit up and turn over.

I'm still wearing my bra and panties. He leans back on his sleeping bag fully dressed, but he holds his head and shoulders up with his stomach contracted. He must want to see what I'll do.

I turn over to face him—and some kind of blast goes off in my mind. I want him. I want all of him. I want more of him than I can take in one lifetime.

He's giving me permission to touch him—and suck him—and take him to the stars just like he took me.

I can't waste this opportunity.

I climb on top of him, take one look at his swollen package, and I know this is right.

I straddle his hips in my panties and ride down on his knob. I dive in and kiss him once. His body looks intoxicating like this with all his muscles contracted.

I only kiss him once and then crawl down his neck mauling him in rabid hunger. I want to devour every part of him.

I dart my hands under his shirt and get another spike of blistering desire when I feel how hard and chiseled his body is. I want to drool all over him while I ride him to kingdom come—but he didn't invite me to do that.

He gasps when I touch him. That sets me off on another wild rollercoaster ride of excitement and ravenous need.

I drag my hungry mouth down his neck to the top of his shirt. He's still wearing his jacket—and he didn't invite me to undress him.

I gnaw down his chest, but his shirt gets in the way. I pull it up as far as his ribs and dive underneath to sink my hot, wet mouth onto his stomach.

Chapter 22: Allison

Caleb's breath catches in his throat and he groans again when I crawl down him toward his belt. His bulge pulsates under his jeans. God, he feels so good like that!

I bite down in big, hot, salivating kisses on his stomach while I yank his belt open. I want to feel his thickness flooding my mouth.

He groans again and his hand flies to my hair. "Yeah, baby," he breathes. "Come on."

I love the way he sounds. He wants this so bad and I'm about to give it to him.

I pull his belt open and unzip his fly. He takes his hand off my head just long enough to pull his shorts down.

His shaft falls out into my face, but before I can suck it into my mouth, his hand clamps in my hair and holds me off.

I gasp and pant in blatant hunger, but he doesn't let me near his prick. It wavers right there in front of my face—so close and yet out of reach.

He controls my head and steers his shaft closer. "Do you want that, baby? Is that what you want?"

I moan in agony trying to stick out my tongue to get near it, but he pulls it away from me.

"No, baby," he whispers. "Not yet."

I sob in torment and then moan when he drags it across my cheek and even my lips, but he won't let me do more than that.

Before I can protest, he pulls me away, shoves me off him, and rolls me onto my back again. He plants his other hand on my chest to hold me down on the floor.

I catch one glimpse—just enough to see that he's pulled up his shorts again. He won't let me near him—not yet.

I collapse sobbing in pathetic defeat in front of him, but before I can start feeling sorry for myself, he strokes his hand up between my legs and rubs me though my panties.

I yelp and then writhe again when he starts touching me. This touch feels so much more blistering hot. It thrills me out of my mind.

I spread my legs trying to get his fingers inside me, but he won't do anything more than rub me. He circles my clitoris and propels me into the stratosphere.

I scream as the first wave breaks. I want to shriek at him and beg him to take me. I want to unload on him how much I need him, but he already knows.

Those words keep spiraling through my mind as I convulse and thrash on the floor in the throes of one cataclysm after another. What is he doing to me?

Every climax he gives me makes me want him more. I need him more than I ever thought possible.

What will happen to me when this night is over? How can my life ever go back to the way it was?

I don't want to go back to the way it was. I don't want to go back to a world where I'm not with him.

Needing him feels like it might actually be good for me—like I need air and food and water to keep living.

I need him. I know that. My life isn't worth shit without him. My life is empty and meaningless without this—whatever this is between u s.

He brings me to such a pitch of ecstasy that I don't even know half of what I'm thinking and feeling. I can't stop winding up and crashing down into seas of pleasure when he keeps playing with me.

I'm still convulsing on the ground in broken screams when he sits up, pulls off my panties, and rolls over between my legs.

He buries his face in my flesh and sends me catapulting into another dizzy climax right there.

I scream with all my might as the heat burns me to the core. His fingers find me and blast me apart when he plunges inside me.

He attacks my flesh in animal bites that spike me out of my mind again and again. I lie splayed on the ground with my thighs spread around his face as he reduces me to a puddle of agonized shrieks and sobs.

He keeps going on and on until I can't see straight. I roll from side to side just trying to survive all the pleasure he's giving me. I don't know who I am or where I am or what I'm doing or why.

I only know I'm with him. I'm going where he's taking me—which is into outer space.

My rational brain shuts down and rides the train of all these orgasms blasting me apart. Where will it end? Maybe he'll never end. Maybe he'll never stop. Maybe he'll keep doing this until there's nothing left of me but one big quivering nerve.

I'm still lying there a trembling wreck when he leans back, rises on his knees, and glares down at me while he pulls off his clothes.

He yanks off his jacket and then peels his shirt off over his head. He looks even bigger, more muscular, and chiseled like this. The shadows coming through the tent set off every cleft and ridge in his powerful chest, arms, shoulders, and midsection.

He throws his clothes aside, strips down his jeans, and then sits down on his sleeping back to take everything off.

I'm too far gone even to speculate about what he's about to do. I wish he would have let me undress him—and touch him all over—and stroke him the way he stroked me.

I guess he has his own way of how he wants to do this.

He takes off his clothes, rotates onto his hands and knees above me, and looks down at me with all that fiery intensity. "Touch me, baby. Touch me the way you want to."

My heart cracks when my hands come to rest on his chest—and then I glide all over him feeling every inch of his skin. A fine carpet of dark hair covers his chest and plunges down in an inward-pointing arrow to his stomach.

I caress his chest, his stomach, up to his armpits, his arms and shoulders, and around to his back.

I whimper in so much emotional desire when I touch his neck and face. Tears come to my eyes when I stroke his hair and down to his cheeks. He means so much to me. I don't want this to end. I don't want to stop feeling this way.

I don't know if I can handle it if he tells me to just go back to being his crewmate tomorrow when this is all over.

I want to hold him against me and feel all his heat pumping into me, but I want this more. I want to look into his eyes and let him see how much he means to me. I love him. That's the truth.

My mouth wrenches out of control when I think that, but I can't tell him. He probably doesn't want to hear that.

I caress him all over his upper body and then down to his hard, bare ass. His ass and thighs are just as muscular as the rest of him—and then my hand closes on his rigid shaft.

He groans and his eyes sink shut just for a moment when I take hold of him and start stroking.

"Oh, yeah, baby," he husks. "That's so good. Yeah.....That's so good."

He breaks off in another broken gasp through his nose. He flexes to shove his meat into my hand.

I stroke down his length.....and then he leans in.

I spread my legs for him and steer him into my waiting channel. All this playing around gets me hot, wet, and tingling to welcome him in.

I guide him in and he pumps in deep and true with strong, forceful, determined strokes.

I can't look away from his eyes. He holds me spellbound as his thickness fills me in a very different way.

He doesn't escalate—not right away. He keeps the same slow, steady rhythm.

His strokes drive all the way in and fill me to the breaking point, but he winds me up at an easier, almost hypnotic rate.

I barely notice the energy rising until I lie panting and shivering underneath him.

I stare up at him and he stares down at me from directly above—right where he can see every tremor in my face and body.

His shoulders loom over me in all their power. His body flexes with tight, hard muscle each time he contracts his abs to drill into me.

I feel my hot juices flowing over him. Every stroke brings another torrent to bathe his shaft and gush down my ass. My flesh squishes and molds around him each time he slots in and grinds his bones against mine to penetrate me deeper than deep.

I keep touching him. I never want to stop touching him. I caress his body, grab his ass to pull him in, and touch his cheeks and hair.

Every part of him feels masterful, exquisite, and carved out of marble. His darkness enthralls me as his body propels me into another dimension—a dimension where nothing exists but him bringing me to this tremulous crescendo of feeling and pleasure.

I waver on the crest of a huge orgasm, but somehow, his eyes hold me there. Does he want to command me to do it? Does he want me to wait until he releases me for his pleasure?

Just at that moment, he shifts his weight to one arm, raises one of my legs, rotates it sideways, and straddles my leg to drill into me from a different angle.

I still lie on my back where he can look down into my eyes, but the new angle creates a cascade of energy that explodes beyond my control.

I scream again and contort onto my side as the explosion hits.

My screams seem to set him off. He unleashes all the brutal power on me that he's been holding back all this time.

He bends over so he can glare right down into my eyes, holds my leg in that position—the perfect position to hit all my most sensitive spots—and slams into me with unbelievable ferocity.

He doubles his speed—triples his speed. He jackhammers me so hard I can't see straight. I can't think. I can only lie here erupting in one catastrophic climax after another.

I spasm all over the place and my slippery, fizzing honey gushes around his mighty shaft. I can't stop the waves of brutal pleasure tearing me to pieces right now.

He angles a little farther back and spanks into my ass extra hard. He pounds me across the tent.

Just when I think I can't take any more of this, he pushes me all the way over and rolls me onto my front.

I collapse there whining and careening out of my mind with continuous bursts of light going off in my mind and body. I can't come down even after he pulls out of me.

He doesn't let me rest even for a second, though. He falls on top of me, pins me under his weight the way he pinned me against the tree, and slides into me from behind.

He straddles my thighs with his and holds my legs together. The added pressure and sensation send me into another screaming tornado of so much bliss that I can't function.

I struggle as much against myself as against him. He grabs me, holds me down, and piledrives into me again and again.

His hips smack my wet ass with each stroke and bring more juicy goodness pouring out of me.

I can only stare into the darkness in front of me and shriek out all this pleasure I never let myself feel before. It took him to release it in ways I never thought possible.

His husky breath rasps in my ear. Those sounds rise to a guttural roar until he pounds in extra hard and his hot load floods me with so much heat that I can't stand it.

I scream in one last escalating peak of torturous pleasure before he collapses on top of me.

Chapter 23: Caleb

I wilt in sagging exhaustion on top of Allison, close my eyes, and let my mouth and teeth sink into her neck from behind.

My shaft throbs and pulsates in her molten channel. I can't stop shaking and trembling all over as one agonizing spasm after another shoots the last of my load inside her.

She lies under me whimpering in broken agony. I may have made a big mistake by doing it with her as hard as I did, but I thought at the time that she enjoyed it.

If I was wrong, I'm screwed.

I can't think about that right now because her channel keeps clenching around my shaft and milking me to swell and eject into her even when there's nothing left in my tank.

She feels mind-blowingly delicious. Every part of her makes my nuts ache to do it with her again.

I didn't even ask if she's on any birth control, but I can't even bring myself to care about that right now.

She responds so beautifully to everything I do. I love hearing her moan and beg me to take her. I love it when she says my name and tells me she needs me.

This hot, dripping honey on my shaft right now.....she loved it. She peaked for me. I can't get enough of hearing her like that.

She lies under me with her head turned to the side. She grimaces in the last ebbs of bliss as she sobs and whines in torturous pleasure.

I want to put my arms around her and hold her all night long. I want to cherish her, but somehow, I always wind up dominating her and making her beg and scream for me to treat her like an animal.

Is it possible that she wants that? She's beyond hot.

My shaft spasms again when I think about the way she went after me with her mouth. She would have sucked me to the ends of the Earth if I only let her.

Just lying on top of her like this—holding her down in such an animalistic position—it makes me hard enough to do it with her again.

I can't—not now. I need to ease off and let her rest. I don't know what she's capable of or even what she wants. I can't control her all the time. I don't even want to.

I want her to enjoy herself. I want her to do what she wants to do. I won't be able to find out what that is if I'm the one always telling her what to do. I don't even want to tell her what to do.

I pry myself off her and try to kiss her, but this isn't the best angle.

Her head lies twisted upward in a suggestive tilt facing the tent wall. She looks tortured and brutalized like this.

I shouldn't get turned on by seeing her like this. I should take it easier on her.

I pull away and a rush of hot fluid follows me out of her channel. She sobs louder when I pull out and her whole body racks with tremors. Poor thing. I should take better care of her.

I topple over onto my sleeping bag and pull it open to get inside. "Come over here, baby," I tell her. "Let me keep you warm."

She takes a long time to pull herself together. When she finally does it, her face contorts in something like agony.

She won't make eye contact with me. Does she regret what we just did? Does she hate me for treating her the way I did?

I want to hold her and make it better. I want to kiss her and somehow make her understand how much I care about her.

I get a rude shock when she climbs on top of me, straddles me the way she did before, and starts kissing me like a goddamn raving animal.

She attacks my mouth so much harder than I ever attacked hers. She snatches at my lips and tongue, invades my mind with blistering kisses, and rides me so hard she makes me roar out loud.

The sudden rush of sensation stiffens my shaft in a split second. All the energy of a minute ago erupts back to life as never before. She won't leave me alone.

Her hands grope all over me. She strokes my chest and stomach, rakes her fingers up my thighs, and grabs my jaw to steer me deeper into her kisses.

I grab a handful of her hair to try to slow her down, but that only sends her into another epic burst of madness.

She rips off my mouth and dives into my neck kissing, biting, and licking me out of control.

I gasp when she mouths my ear with one scorching breath—and then she's going after my neck again.

My clothes aren't here to protect me from her—or maybe the fact that I'm not dressed is making her go off the rails like this.

She mauls me down my chest, bites my nipples, and her hot breath leaves a trail of fire to my stomach.

There's no stopping her this time, and in seconds, her mouth closes on me. I gasp in one ragged lungful of air before her strong, hot mouth starts to suck. Holy crap, I'm in trouble.

I grab her hair again, but that only makes her more ravenous. She sucks deep and hard. Every throb, spasm, and twitch of my meat in her mouth sends her over the edge and makes her more enthusiastic.

I follow her movements and stare down at her in blank shock. No woman has ever sucked me like this before. She goes at me like she's starving for it.

I can't take much more of this. Her lips glide up and down my shaft on a river of saliva mixed with our combined juices.

Her hands caress me all over my chest and stomach while she inhales me. She plays with my nuts and even fiddles with my armpits like she's in heaven.

I keep my head and shoulders up so I can see her. I have to keep my eyes open for every second of this. Please, Dear God, let me die right now.

She excites me too much. I feel myself getting ready to explode in her mouth. I shouldn't, but she's enjoying herself too much. I don't have the heart to stop her.

I wouldn't want to stop her if she wants me to explode in her mouth. Maybe that's what she has been waiting for all night. Maybe she wanted it outside. Maybe she wanted it earlier when I stopped her from sucking me. Who am I to deny her that?

She doesn't stop—not once. She keeps going, and the next time her delicate fingers so much as graze my nuts, I erupt into her mouth.

I clench my fists in her hair, roar out in an agony of pleasure, and try not to pump into her mouth too deep or too hard.

I might have done it anyway, though, but she doesn't seem to care.

She opens her mouth wider and swallows my load down to the last drop.

I roar at her in wordless fury as my body unloads into her. I can't stop it. I don't want to stop it and she doesn't seem to want to stop it, either.

I collapse back on my sleeping bag shaking and groaning. Jesus Christ, what have I gotten myself into with this woman? I am in way over my head here.

Before I even have time to catch my breath, she climbs on top of me, nuzzles into my neck, and straddles me exactly the same way—but not the same way.

She pushes my quivering shaft inside her and starts rocking for the ages. I yell out as another brutal spasm hits me—and then all my blood rushes to my prick.

She makes me so damn hard that it hurts. I can't take it anymore, but she shows no sign of slowing down.

She bites my earlobe once, kisses me, and pushes herself up to sit straight on top of me.

Her eyes swim with intoxicated madness—and then she bursts into such a magnificent smile of pure happiness.

She stretches her arms behind her back, unclasps her bra, and takes it off for the first time.

She doesn't stop riding me even once when she lays her bra aside on her pile of clothes, turns around to rest her hands on my chest, and pumps her hips into me in a rhythmic galloping motion to ride us both to the stars.

I stare up at her in dazed shock. She is so magnificently beautiful sitting there with her breasts exposed and her hair cascading all over her shoulders.

Her smokey eyes shine with so much poignant emotion when she touches me. She doesn't attack me or maul me. Her hands caress my chest and stomach. She pushes a little harder on the back stroke to drill herself down on my spike.

She keeps smiling at me with so much tortured affection. Is that love? Is she looking at me with love?

Her features twist and tears spring to her eyes when she looks down at me. Her mouth won't stay in one position for long, but I've never seen her so happy—not even when she was laughing at my jokes.

My hands rise to her breasts.....and glide down to her voluptuous hips.....and to her beautiful face. She looks so dreamy like this—like something out of my most fevered sexual fantasies.

She's real, though. She's right here on top of me riding my prick to make herself scream with ecstasy again.

Her smell overwhelms me with sweetness. Her inner muscles carry me away to a distant world of bliss and fulfillment until she sags over on top of me still bleating and whining in another catastrophic outburst of orgasmic rapture.

I pull the sleeping bag around both of us, but I can't zip it closed when she's straddling me like this.

I shift her to the side and roll her off me so I can hold her.

She keeps twitching and jerking when I fold her in my arms, kiss her hair, and draw her head down on my shoulder.

Chapter 24: Caleb

I wake up out of a hazy dream—but it wasn't a dream. Allison lies in my arms with her fragrant hair spilling all over my chest.

Her arms clasp around my body. She's thrown one thigh over my leg. Her slit and thighs still feel wet from last night.

I stare up at the tent ceiling and use this moment of silence to think. I don't know how she's going to react when she wakes up.

She might want to go home and forget this ever happened. She might want us to go back to being co-workers and nothing else.

I don't want that. I know that now. I want more. I want to keep her for myself.

Now, in this moment, I can finally admit that to myself.

I wanted that from the beginning. I wanted that from the first moment I ever met her.

I didn't let myself think it while I knew she belonged to another man. I would never intrude on something like that—and things got so complicated after that.

Now I know. Last night confirmed it. I want her. The only question is if I can get her.

I have to be careful not to push her too far. She made it pretty clear last night that she doesn't think she's ready for another relationship.

I have to be okay with that. I am okay with that. I don't want her getting involved in something unless she's one hundred percent enthusiastic about it.

I sure as hell wouldn't want her to get together with me if she wasn't one hundred percent enthusiastic about it.

I'll just have to proceed with care. I have to see how she feels and take the consequences of that decision.

I lie still thinking it over. If she decides to leave, I'll stay out here another day like I originally planned to, just to get my head screwed on straight before I go back to work.

Then I'll walk back into the firehouse as if none of this ever happened.

No one ever has to find out we spent a wild night of passion doing it in a tent in the woods. I can put it out of my mind exactly the same way I put Clay out of my mind.

She stirs in a little while, groans, and then sinks down on top of me before she wakes all the way up. She finally rolls off to one side onto her back and runs her fingers through her hair.

I take that opportunity to unzip the sleeping bag and sit up. "Do you want some coffee?" I ask.

"Um...okay....yeah.....thanks," she mumbles. She sounds like she's still half asleep.

I get busy lighting my camp stove, boiling the water, and adding the coffee to my French press. I'm a coffee freak. So sue me.

Out of nowhere, her hand comes to rest on my bare back. I stiffen for a minute and then relax into it. I forgot I had my shirt off.

She leaves her hand resting lightly there while I work. I don't know what to think or feel from that touch. It feels....intimate. Does it mean something?

I pour the boiling water into the press and set it aside while I start making breakfast. I pull the eggs out of my pack.

I'm in the middle of scrambling them when she asks in a shaky voice, "Caleb?"

"Yeah?" I ask over my shoulder.

"Does last night mean we're done?" Her voice breaks with so much anguish that I can't stand it. "Does it mean we're going to walk away and never see each other again?"

I spin around and the bottom drops out of my world when I see tears in her eyes. Her face distorts in misery.

I dive on top of her and try to kiss her. "Hey, baby!" I murmur. "I loved last night! Do you know how long I've dreamed of this?"

"I can't let go of you!" she wails. "I can't just walk away and say it didn't mean anything.....I love you!" She bursts into tears. "I'm sorry! I know you don't want to hear that, but I can't help it! I just admire you so much! I can't think of any guy I would rather get with.....but I know you don't want that with me!"

"Stop it!" I breathe. "I do want it with you! I want it more than anything! I wanted it from day one, but you were with someone else, so I had to back off. I didn't want to step on your toes by telling you." I put my arms around her. "Don't cry. I love you, too."

She breaks down in racking sobs and huddles in my arms. I kiss the top of her head. The sound of her sobbing makes me want to cry, too. God, she's so precious!

I never should have made her doubt the way I feel about her. I should have had that conversation with her before we spent the night together.

It's too late now. We just have to have that conversation now, but right then, the butter starts sputtering in the frying pan.

I have to sit up and add the eggs to the pan before it burns. She lies back in the sleeping bag. She pulls herself together and sits up by the time I finish making breakfast and serving coffee.

I only have one mug, so I serve her coffee first. I also only have one plate and one fork, so I eat with my fingers from the frying pan.

I only brought enough for one person, but I satisfy myself with half my usual breakfast so she can have the other half.

She eats it in silence. I take the plate and mug away from her when she finishes.

I pull my clothes toward me. "I'm going to go outside and wash up. I'll be right back."

I get dressed, take my camp stove outside, and get some water from the nearby stream to wash my dishes. By the time I come back, she stands outside the tent fully dressed with her hair in a ponytail.

"You're rostered on to work tomorrow, aren't you?" she asks while she watches me work.

"Yes, but I'm on the afternoon shift. You're on in the morning, aren't you?"

She nods. "How do you want to handle that?"

"Handle what—us working together?"

"Yes," she replies.

"We'll handle it the way we always have—by acting perfectly professional around each other. I don't see that anything has changed in our working relationship. Do you?"

She looks away. "I guess not."

"Is something wrong?" I ask. "Do you have a problem with anything I did last night? Please tell me now if you did."

She won't look at me. "I don't have a problem with anything you did last night. I loved every second of it. I just wish I knew where we stood. That's all."

I don't answer. I'm pretty certain where I stand. She just told me where she stands, but apparently, she needs some more definite confirmation that I feel the same way.

I finish the dishes and put everything away. I come out of the tent and find her still standing there.

I take her hand. "Come with me, baby." I leave my tent and all my gear and lead her away into the woods.

She follows me in silence. The tension coming from her spikes off the charts. She doesn't know what to think or what to do.

I actually love that she's so fragile around me. She really does need me. She wasn't just saying that in the sexual sense of wanting me to do it with her. She meant it literally.

I lead her back to the main path. We climb over the fallen tree and I escort her all the way back to the parking lot.

I take her over to her car, cup her cheeks in both hands, and stare deep into her eyes. "I want you to get into your car, drive home, get your uniforms and whatever else you need for work tomorrow, and meet me back at my place. Do you understand? Do you know the address?"

She nods. Her eyes well up with tears again and her face twists all over the place.

"I want you to stay with me," I tell her. "I want to take you home and never let you leave. Do you understand now? I want you—all of you. Where are you living right now, anyway?"

"We bought a house...me and Clay.....we just sold it......I've been in a temporary rental while I decide what to do.....but I already made the decision to stay in Howe.....I had a conversation with Duke about it....I just haven't found anywhere else to live."

"You're living with me as of this morning. Understand? Get your stuff out of the rental and drive over to my house. You can work on moving the rest of the way out of the rental later."

Her whole face crunches up into a mass of agony. "Really?"

"Yes, really. You're all I've ever wanted since the moment I laid eyes on you. If you say you love me and you don't want to let me go, then I'll never give you up. Come home with me and stay with me. You don't have to worry about anything else. I swear it."

"What about......what about Duke?"

"You let me deal with Duke—and everyone else at the firehouse. You just keep doing your job and staying on the straight and narrow. You'll be fine. We both will. We'll do it together—just like everyone else at the firehouse. Okay?"

She nods again, but she won't stop crying. I see so much history and lost potential in her tears.

I kiss her on the forehead and push her toward her car. "Go now, baby. I'll see you at home in a little while."

I stand back and watch while she gets into her car and drives away. She's still sobbing her eyes out when she vanishes down the mountain.

I head back up the trail to my campsite and get busy breaking it all down. I pack it out to my truck, throw everything in the back, and drive home. I have a lot of work to do before I have to go to work tomorrow.

Chapter 25: Allison

I can't stop shaking when I park my car at the curb outside Caleb's house. He owns a very nice sprawling suburban hacienda on the outskirts of Howe.

He doesn't live in the same neighborhood near the school where most of the firehouse families live. Most of them bought houses close to the school so their kids could walk to school.

Thick trees surround Caleb's house on all sides. It's a wooded spot with acreage between all the houses so they can't see each other.

A curving driveway leads up to the house. Overhanging oak trees surround the front porch. The place looks like something out of a bygone era.

I go through another attack of nervous trembling when I see Caleb's truck parked in the driveway. He goes back and forth between the truck and the garage to put his camping gear away.

I haven't been back in Howe for very long since I left the campsite. He must have packed up and driven straight here after we separated in the parking lot.

I don't know why I'm so nervous—except that he just basically told me to move in with him.

I actually love it when he just flat-out tells me what to do. It makes me feel better—like we both understand that he's so much better at making life decisions than I am. I don't have to wonder if I'm doing the right thing.

If he thinks us moving in together is a good idea, it must be.

He said we would stay on the straight and narrow together. What could be better than that?

Clay never said anything like that to me. He probably didn't know what the straight and narrow was if he could go off the deep end like that.

Neither of us knew what the straight and narrow was back then. I don't know if I would have gotten together with him if I did know.

I wouldn't have hesitated to tell Caleb the truth if I had been on the straight and narrow. Telling him I had a fiancé would have been the very first thing out of my mouth the instant I met him.

I try to shake that thought out of my head. I don't want to think about Clay or the past when I'm sitting here right outside Caleb's front gate.

He sees me from the garage, strides down the driveway toward me, and bends down to the driver's window. "Drive into the driveway and park behind my truck. Don't stay out here on the curb."

I'm shaking too badly to answer. I don't know why. It isn't like anything bad will happen to me here.

Maybe all the nervous exhaustion and sensory overload from last night is finally catching up with me.

I reverse, drive in, and park just as Caleb comes back. "Where's your stuff?" he asks.

"In the trunk." I pop the latch.

He doesn't wait for me even to get out of the car. He lifts my duffel bag out of the trunk, slams it shut, and takes my hand. "Come inside. I'll show you around."

He leads me up the porch. I feel like I'm stepping back in time when I enter a high, arched living room with long, sweeping wings going off to each side.

Tall windows cover the opposite walls on both sides and look out on an even more densely wooded yard rolling away to wild, overgrown acreage out back.

A massive stone fireplace dominates one wall of the living room with a flat-screen TV on the wall above the mantelpiece. A broad, luxurious kitchen extends from the other side of the living room.

The kitchen is almost another room unto itself. A tiled, glassed-in dining room sits beyond the kitchen. More enormous windows adjoin the rest of the curved wall overlooking the backyard.

"This place is incredible!" I gasp.

"Not too bad, huh?" He turns aside. "Come over here."

He leads the way into one of the side wings. Sunshine streams through big windows in a long veranda down the front of the house.

This side faces the front yard and the road, but too many trees block off the front perimeter. No one would be able to see in.

The veranda opens into multiple bedrooms, each one set up for guests.

"How can you afford this on a firefighter's salary?" I whisper. "This place is like a mansion."

"I bought it when it was all rundown, overgrown, and forgotten. No one wanted it—and it was packed to the ceiling with trash. Those big windows in the living room weren't there. Those walls were completely rotten and falling down. I installed those windows and fixed up the kitchen and the dining room. The rest of it is original." He blushes when he sees my reaction. "This is nothing. You should see Billy's house. That guy is an absolute madman."

He leads the way into the master bedroom. It's flippin' enormous. It's bigger than the living room of the house Clay and I bought.

I can tell right away that a man lives here. A giant carved wooden sleigh bed sits on one side.

The bedspread and all the furnishings follow an old, burnished, natural brown-and-tan color scheme with a few hints of white thrown in here and there.

An enormous curve-backed leather couch sits in front of another bank of windows facing the east side of the property. A woven brown velvet throw blanket hangs over the couch's swooping arms and button-studded seat.

An equally impressive carved mahogany dresser stands oppose the bed with a bunch of Caleb's personal effects on top of it and a mirror on the wall above.

He throws my duffel bag on the bed. "You can stay here and make yourself at home. I'm kind of eccentric in my eating habits, so please don't be offended if I forget to cook or eat at a specific time. Sometimes I get busy with other things and forget to eat, so I'm all over the place. I'm fine with it if you want to set up a more regular schedule, but you might need to remind me if you want me to do anything."

I turn around slowly to look at him. I can't believe this. I hardly dare let myself fully accept that he really wants me to come live with him—here.

I never could have envisioned a place like this when Clay and I bought that house. It never occurred to me to buy something as unique and dripping with charm as this.

I find myself staring at Caleb with new eyes. He must be even more exceptional than I thought if he lives somewhere like this.

The deafening silence makes me realize that Caleb is waiting for me to say something intelligent about the fact that I just moved in with him.

He cocks his head to study me. "Why don't you unpack your stuff and start getting ready for tomorrow? You should probably get to sleep early tonight to make up for last night."

I go over to the bed in a trance. Whatever he thinks is a good idea is good enough for me.

I sit down on the bed, pull my duffel bag toward me, and start taking things out of it. I don't have a regular place to live, so I'll just treat this place as the next best thing until I get used to how palatial and luxurious it is.

I pull out my uniforms, my pajamas, my toothbrush and toothpaste, and my hairbrush, blow dryer, and makeup for tomorrow.

I'll need to ask Caleb where the bathroom is, but I don't seem to be thinking clearly at all. I really need to crash—and I don't even know if I'll be able to do that.

How will Caleb and I be able to live together without tearing each other's clothes off every minute of the day?

I'm still rummaging around in my duffel bag when he comes over to me, closes both hands around my face, and lifts my head so I have no choice but to look at him.

His eyes overflow with so much emotion. He really means it. He loves me. He didn't just say that because I said it.

My throat constricts when I realize. This is real. I'm living with him. We spent the night together—and now we're going to be together.

"Do you want me, baby?" he murmurs.

Tears well up in my eyes and my throat constricts. I can barely make myself heard. "I need you so much, Caleb!"

"You're mine," he breathes. "You're mine and I'm going to keep you here as long as you want to stay. Do you understand? No one is ever going to take you away from me."

I can't stand being this far away from him. I throw my arms around his waist, bury my face in his stomach, and hug him tight. I can't help but shed tears into his shirt. I never thought anything like this would happen to me.

He cradles the back of my head in one hand and rubs my back with the other.

He pulls away first, kisses me once, and points at me while he backs away. "I gotta go finish putting my gear in the garage. Unpack your stuff and settle in. I'll be back in a minute."

Chapter 26: Caleb

I come in from the garage, go into the kitchen, and make a thorough inspection of the fridge, freezer, and pantry.

I'm going to have to get my act together, now that Allison is coming to live here.

Following the straight and narrow meant something different when I lived alone. No one knew or cared if I ate at all hours.

I'll have to change that, now that she's here.

I need to go to the grocery store and get some supplies. I suppose I'll have to talk to her about what she wants to eat, when she wants to eat, and how she wants to do everything.

She might be one of those strict, three-meals-a-day-by-the-clock types. I'm cool with that. It just means I'll have to level up my game, but that's all part of the straight and narrow path.

I'll also have to talk to her about the whole birth control thing and sound her out about how she feels about us potentially having kids.

I make a shopping list and go into the bedroom to tell her where I'm going.

I stop when I see her sprawled on my bed, sound asleep. I have to smile down at her. Aw, how sweet. I wore her out.

My heart bursts when I look at her. This house is going to become a very different place with a woman living in it.

I'm going to take care of her. I'm going to make sure she has what she needs so she never feels the need to leave.

I know she was loyal to Clay. I'm never going to put her through something like that again.

I have to angle my truck around her car to get out of the driveway. Then I drive to the store and put everything away before I go check on her.

She sleeps for a long time. She didn't even get a chance to put her stuff away before she passed out.

She's still asleep at six o'clock in the evening and she has to go back to work at seven o'clock tomorrow morning.

I make some tacos for both of us, take them into the bedroom, and start hanging her uniforms in the closet.

I hang her stuff on the opposite side of the closet from my uniforms so we can tell everything apart. I leave my casual clothes between them so we can tell whose stuff is whose.

I'm in the middle of moving my underwear, socks, and T-shirts into fewer drawers so she can have some to herself. I catch myself smelling her underwear and bras when I put them in the drawers. Mmm. She's exquisite.

She wakes up while I'm folding her T-shirts. She sighs in her sleep and then jolts upright when she sees where she is.

I sit down next to her and rub her leg while her wild eyes skate around the room. "It's all right," I tell her. "You're at my house. Remember? You're all right. You fell asleep. Here. Eat some dinner."

I put the plate of tacos on the bed in front of her. She blinks at the food and then at the room while her brain catches up with reality.

I bring my plate over and sit next to her. She looks down at her plate and doesn't engage with me while we both eat.

She might still be half-asleep—or she might still not feel totally comfortable with the fact that she's here at all.

"Listen to me, baby," I tell her. "Tomorrow, while you're on the morning shift, I'm going to go to the city jail and see Clay."

Her head shoots up and she stares at me with huge eyes. "What for?"

"I'm going to tell him you and I are together now. He deserves to hear it from one of us and we don't know when the Department of Corrections will transfer him upstate. I have tomorrow off, so I'll go talk to him."

She gulps to swallow her food and looks back down at her plate.

"You okay?" I ask. "This is the right thing to do. You don't have to see him. If he has anything nasty to say, he can say it to me."

"If you think it's the right thing to do, then I trust you," she mumbles. "I couldn't face him."

"You know this is the right thing to do. We have no reason to hide it from him. He would be furious if he found out we didn't tell him while he was still here in Howe."

"I don't know what the right thing to do is anymore," she murmurs. "I guess that's the point of all of this. The one thing I learned from all of this is that I can't trust myself to do the right thing when it needs to be done. If you think us getting together is a good idea, then I trust you to make that decision for both of us. If you think we should move in together, then you know better than I do if that's the right thing to do or not. You're much better at this kind of thing than I am."

I stare at her trying to take all of that in. "You have to trust yourself. You're a paramedic. You couldn't start second-guessing all your decisions."

"I don't mean as a paramedic. I mean everything outside of that. Me being a paramedic is the only thing about my life that I understand and can rely on. You said I wasn't ready to get into a relationship and you were right about that. You told me to go make peace with Clay and own up to the part I played in what happened. You were right about that, too. If you think I'm ready for all of this, then I trust you. You have a much better perspective on whether I'm ready than I do. I would have kept living alone. I never would have tried to go out with you again. I don't think I would have tried with anyone—or at least it would have taken a lot longer before I decided I was ready."

I blink at her in shock. "So you don't think you're ready for this?"

"I don't think I'm ready and I don't think I'm unready. I think you're better qualified to make these decisions than I am."

Now it's my turn to gulp. Do I really want that responsibility? "What makes me better qualified to make these decisions than you are?"

"Because you didn't make a series of disastrous life decisions that completely ruined one man's life and very nearly cost another his. I did that. You flirted with a girl you thought was attractive. I don't call that a serious lapse in judgment—not like someone failing to mention that she was engaged to one man when another was trying to get her to go out with him and then lying about it to twist the situation in her favor. I call that a serious lapse in judgment."

I cast my gaze down at my plate. "So if I decided you weren't ready for a relationship, you would walk away from me and not try to get me back?"

Tears well up in her eyes when she nods at me. "If you really thought this relationship was no good for us, then yes, I would accept your decision. You've been right about pretty much everything else. I trust you. I trust you a lot more than I trust myself."

I'm not sure how I feel about that, but I'm not ready to let her go. "How about we continue with this until one of us sees some reason why we shouldn't? If you see something about this that doesn't seem right to you, you'll tell me and vice versa. Then we'll talk about it and decide what to do about it."

"Okay," she replies. "I just want you to know how I feel about it. If you think going to see Clay is the right thing, then I trust you on that, too."

I lean over the bed and kiss her. "Thank you. I believe it is the right thing. I would want to know if I was in his place—especially since he's right here in the same town with us. We should tell him before he ships o ut."

She mumbles, "Okay," into her tacos and keeps eating.

I can't tell if my decision gives her any relief or not.

She finishes first. "Could you please tell me where the bathroom is?" she asks.

I point to the opposite side of the bedroom. "Over there."

Chapter 27: Caleb

Allison leaves her plate on the bed and goes to the bathroom. I stuff the last of my tacos into my mouth, take the plates to the dishwasher, and return to find her putting the rest of her stuff away.

I sprawl on the bed to watch her. "What do you want to do about meals?" I ask.

"What about them?" she asks over her shoulder.

"Do you want to have them regularly and set times or do you want us to forage like wild beasts?"

She laughs without turning around. "I wondered when your natural sense of humor would come back."

"I guess I've been in kind of a funk since some lunatic tried to shoot me."

"I call it a growing, maturing process. I've never been a stickler for set mealtimes, either—what with always being on shift at the firehouse and constantly getting called out to emergencies at all hours. I've just gotten in the habit of eating whenever—and Clay never ate at regular times, either. He got into the same habit during his intern days."

"Then I guess we can just keep doing that."

She comes back over to the bed, starts organizing her makeup and hair products, and puts them on the dresser next to my things.

"We could start out that way, or if one of us wants to arrange a more formal sit-down dinner, we can do that, too," I suggest. "And we could go out to eat sometimes."

"That's a good idea."

She's in the middle of stacking her makeup on my dresser.

"Baby?" I ask.

"Yeah?" she asks over her shoulder.

"Are you on birth control?"

She spins around fast and stares at me. Her face goes through a series of expressions—mostly of blank terror. What does she think—that I'm going to bust her for that?

She gulps again. "Yes," she chokes. "I am. Did you want me to go off of it?"

"How do you feel about that? Did you and Clay plan to go off of it?"

"We planned to wait a year—after we moved up here—just to see if things worked out between us. Then....we planned.....that I would go off of it."

I nod. "Why don't we do the same thing? We'll wait a year and then talk about whether we're ready for you to go off of it."

She gulps again. This whole thing must scare the pants off her.

I should have realized. I should have taken it slower. I didn't mean to push her into a situation that would cause her so much distress.

I hold out my hand to her. "Come here, baby."

She comes toward me, takes my hand, and lets me pull her between my knees. I kiss her—only once and very gently.

"Everything is going to work out," I tell her. "If you don't want to do something, all you have to do is tell me. I'll never make you do anything you don't want to do—not ever."

Her eyes race around the room and her voice cracks with buried emotion again. "You've always been so kind to me—much better than I deserve!"

"You deserve all of this. You deserve to be happy."

She looks down at the floor. Is she hiding tears again? She compresses her lips.

"What's wrong? What's bothering you?"

"I really want......I really want......to have a family with you! I shouldn't even be telling you this when I just moved in here...."

"Why shouldn't you tell me? Don't you know how much I want to hear that you love me?"

"I do love you! I just want to do what's best for you! I don't want to screw this up!"

"Then don't screw it up. Stay on the straight and narrow. If anyone asks or tries to flirt with you, tell them you're already with someone. It's that simple."

She raises her hand to hastily wipe a tear off her cheek. "I am so sorry, Caleb—about all of it! I wish I could take it all back! It would almost be worth spending the rest of my life with Clay just to make it so none of this ever happened."

"Okay, stop it!" I breathe. "I don't want you to apologize to me about that anymore. It's over and done with. It's in the past. It's an interesting story about how you and I wound up together. That's all."

She swallows hard and doesn't answer. She won't look at me. God, she must be so ashamed of what she did. I had no idea it was bothering her this much.

I pull her toward me. "Come here and get in bed. You're exhausted. You need to go back to sleep."

I pull her down on the bed, scoot back against the cushions, and position her next to me with her head on my chest.

She sinks into me, wraps her arms around me, and settles down, but as soon as she gets into that position, she starts crying again.

"Shh!" I whisper and kiss her hair. "Shhh!"

She doesn't stop for a while. Maybe it will take her longer than I anticipated to get over all of that.

That's okay. I can live with that. Coming to live here is a big adjustment for her—especially after she thought nothing could ever happen between us.

I wait for her to stop crying and then tell her to go change into her pajamas and brush her teeth. I do the same thing, pull down the covers, and we both get in.

I pull her toward me, but she feels different now. She's wearing a white cotton nightdress with tiny roses dotted across the frilly lace upper bodice.

She isn't wearing anything underneath it—not even underwear.

She feels unimaginably sexy when she presses her body against me. I can feel every curve, every soft place, and every inch of her delicious flesh.

I immediately start getting hard when I feel her breasts, her thighs gliding against each other, and her shapely round ass falling perfectly into my hands.

She sighs and then moans when I pull her in and kiss her. She shudders and then pumps her hips against the bulge in my pajama pants.

That little tremor running through her electrifies me. I gotta have her.

My hands can't get enough of her. This flimsy nightgown turns me on even more than the naked body underneath. I can't wait to see her walking around in this and knowing that my jiz is bubbling out of her puffy, swollen slit.

I kiss her for the ages and her mouth opens to meet me. She's so much softer, warmer, and less fevered here than she was in the tent. She was mind-blowingly hot there, too, but this is different.

This is my woman. She's mine. I know that now. I'm taking her in my own bed. She's living in my house.

Nothing stops me from pushing up her nightgown and groping her ass and thighs in both hands.

She slides perfectly over me and straddles me when I pull her on top of me.

She doesn't hesitate at all this time. She sits up, pulls her nightgown off, and sits down on my shaft without any introduction or warmup.

I groan when her muscles clench around me and her hot wetness swallows me.

She throws back her head and arches her back in delicious waves. Her round breasts fall right into my hands when I reach out and grab them.

She rocks and sways to the rhythm of me pumping into her from below. She moans louder and her pace quickens.

In a second, she speeds up to a cantering beat throwing herself down on my spike. She lets out a little cry of excitement each time she thrusts all the way in.

I grab her ass in one hand and her hip in the other. She said she loved what I did with her last night. She wanted it. She really did orgasm all those times.

I want to do all of that with her again, but not now. She looks absolutely stunning sitting on top of me with her head thrown back, her hair spilling all over her shoulders and down her breasts, her hard nipples pointing in my face, and her back arched in pleasure when she feels my slab breaking her apart.

I pull and push her hips faster and harder. She screams once and then rockets into keening, orgasmic cries. Her head falls forward and her mouth falls open in desperate completion.

Her features spasm again and again each time I ram into her. Her channel swells into an even tighter, hotter, moister, more fervent vessel for me.

Her body goes limp in my grasp, but I keep pulling her into my thrusts until she flops forward and collapses on my chest.

I'm nowhere near done with her, though, and I'm still throbbing hard.

I wrap my arms around her and roll her onto her back. She sways and undulates in my grasp. She follows all my movements, and when I arch to drive into her, her eyes roll back in their sockets as another tormenting wave of rapture takes her.

She moans in deep satisfaction. Her body goes all rubbery underneath me....and then her eyes float open.

She swims in a drunken stupor staring up into my eyes with so much rapture and......and love. She loves me. She really does.

She comes to life again and slithers her velvety arms and thighs all over me while I stroke into her.

She caresses her legs up my sides, wraps them around my waist, and then strokes them down to hook her feet behind my ass.

She caresses my chest and wraps her arms around me to pull me down into her beautiful box.

Just when I think my world couldn't get any better, she plunges her hand down between my legs and massages my nuts while I pump into her.

The sensation blasts me into outer space. I never want this to end. She caresses me beyond gently—just enough to give me the greatest pleasure of my life.

I want her to keep doing it, but I want to make her climax even more. I straighten up so she has to let go of me.

She falls back on the bed and I prop myself on my knees so I can wrap her legs around my waist.

I pull her into my thrusts harder....and harder.....and lay my fingers against her clitoris so I can rub her at the same time.

She bursts into a fresh wave of torrential orgasms. She thrashes in my arms so hard I have to hold her in position, but her channel softens and ripens around me like nothing I've ever felt.

Her walls engorge beyond belief. Her deep, cushiony wetness swallows me until I have no choice but to unload into her.

I want to throw back my head and roar out all this passionate release, but I have to see her. I have to see her body writhing in ecstasy in front of me before we both buckle onto the bed.

My eyes swim open and I see Allison lying all naked and glowing on my bed next to me. I almost pass out from the memory of all the times I've done it with her.

I'm going to do it with her a whole lot more times—in every possible way. I'm going to make her scream my name until she can't see straight.

Her skin radiates pure light in the sheen of the bedside lamp. Her body is too perfect. I can't keep my hands off her.

I stroke her beautiful thighs, her perfect round mound, her swooping valley of a stomach, and up to her pendulous breasts lying sideways when she leans against one arm.

She comes to life again as soon as I start touching her, but she doesn't try to touch me in return. She twists onto her back and seethes on the bed in front of me while I touch her.

Christ, I love watching her like this! I love how much my touch excites her.

Her thighs drag against each other with my essence still glistening on her immaculate skin. Her slit swells open with desire when I pass my hand across her mound.

Her nipples stick straight up in the air for me to tease them with little pinches between my fingers.

She keeps turning her head from side to side, grimacing in an agony of desperate longing, and arching her body into my hand.

"Look at me, baby," I tell her. "Look at me and tell me you love me."

She turns her head and her sex-drunk eyes float open to meet mine. "Caleb...." she moans.

"Do you want me, baby?" I ask even though I already know the answer.

She opens her mouth to answer, but I interrupt her by trailing my finger ever-so lightly up her slit. She moans out loud in deep hunger, but I move off just as fast.

"Caleb....please...." she rasps.

"Do you need me in there, baby?" I ask.

She grabs my wrist and tries to get me to finger her, but I have no problem overpowering her.

She doesn't really try to get me to touch her. She just struggles against her own feelings that won't subside—because I won't let them subside.

I could keep playing with her and teasing her all night long. I sure would love to, but she does have to work tomorrow.

I push myself up on my elbow, lean over her, and kiss her long and deep. I know what I'm going to be doing with her every time we have days off together. We're going to get a lot of mileage out of this bed.

I pull away and stroke her cheeks and hair while I bask in the radiant love and longing shining in her eyes.

She gazes up at me with such unashamed passion and heartfelt desire. She never hides anything from me—not even how much I mean to her.

I ease back, sit up, and pick up her nightgown. I help her slide into it and she shimmies it down to her knees.

She lies back on the bed while I pull on my pajama pants and switch off the light.

We both crawl under the covers and I pull her in a second time.

She feels just as dreamy and delicious now as she did before, but it's up to me to make sure she gets the rest she needs.

I close my eyes and let myself relax in the softness of her body cuddling into my arms.

I can dream about her thighs straddling me, her hands gripping my nuts while I impale her, her breasts falling into my face, her thighs surrounding my head while I devour her sweetness, and all those blessed moments yet to come.

They exist in my mind right now and my mind makes them real—as real as if they were actually happening. I can enjoy her in my dreams until those dreams become reality.

Chapter 28: Allison

C aleb leans across the kitchen counter and kisses me. "You better go to work, baby. You don't want to be late."

My eyes dart up to his face. "Did you mean what you said about handling things with Duke and the rest of the crew?"

"Yes, absolutely. I'll talk to him when I start my shift and then I'll tell the rest of the crew. The news will spread through the grapevine and then we'll have to put up with a few weeks of everyone giving us a hard time about it."

I find myself bursting into laughter. "I suppose I should have expected that."

"It's the natural order of things. Just ride it out in good grace and everyone will forget about it. Just look at the others: Keith and Leila, Danny and Emily, Duke and Naomi, Brooke and Billy, Carter and Sophie, Chris and Josh—they all went through it. Now no one even notices it."

"You're right. I guess I'm just nervous about it."

"There's nothing to be nervous about. They're family. They'll be happy for us."

I stand up and take my dishes to the dishwasher. "I better go. Have a good time. I mean.....good luck. *Don't* have a good time."

He makes a face at me over his shoulder. "I'll call you at lunchtime and tell you how things went."

I turn bright red, but we don't have time to talk about it now. I kiss him goodbye and go get in my car.

I still find it difficult to believe that I'm actually living with Caleb in this magnificent house.

I drive away to the firehouse and pretend to go about my business. No one knows the secret I'm carrying around.

Does my body smell like sex? Can anyone see that I did it with Caleb both of my two nights off—and now I'm living with him?

I get through my usual truck checks without anyone finding out. The rest of the crew has their own business to attend to.

We don't get a call all morning. We head up to the breakroom where the paramedics help the firefighters and EMTs with their professional development workbooks.

That seems to be the trend when it comes to killing time in the breakroom. We would make too many snide remarks if we did anything else.

Eleven-thirty rolls around before I remember Caleb saying he would call me at lunchtime.

I get extremely nervous thinking about him meeting with Clay and breaking the news that we're together. I hope Clay doesn't get too nasty about it.

Caleb will be able to handle that much better than I would. I wouldn't trust myself not to get nasty back—which is exactly the mistake that I made last time.

I try to pull out my phone to see if I've gotten any messages from Caleb. I pat down my pockets and realize that I left my phone downstairs in my locker.

I make an excuse and go down there to get it. I'm just on my way out again and I turn off to the stairs when a woman and her young son walk into the garage.

The woman looks like she's about thirty-five, but the years haven't been kind to her. She looks haggard, malnourished, and jumpy. Her skin sags off her bones in papery, almost translucent wrinkles.

She wears her thinning hair in a twisted knot on the back of her head. A long, shapeless, threadbare dress many sizes too big for her hangs off her skeletal frame.

She clings to her son way too tightly. Her bony, fleshless fingers dig into his shoulders. He stares up at me with wide, petrified eyes like he's afraid of me and needs his mother to protect him.

"Can I help you?" I ask as politely as I can.

"I need to see Caleb," the woman tells me.

I stiffen immediately. "He isn't working right at this moment. Can I leave a message to let him know what this is about? He could contact you back."

"Where is he?" she snaps much more harshly. "I'm his wife and this is his son. I need to see him right away."

My heart stops. Caleb lied to me. He moved in on me when he already has a wife and son.

The woman sees my hesitation. "You know where he is, don't you? Tell me right now. I have a right to know where he is."

My mind turns a somersault. "Are you sure we're talking about the right Caleb? He's been living in Howe for years. He never said anything about a...."

"He abandoned us in Crayton!" the woman counters. "He got into a car accident and lost his memory! He doesn't know who he is. He wandered off. We've been looking for him ever since. Now tell me where he is before I call the Police."

I force myself to calm down. I'm supposed to be a professional. "Caleb is off duty at the moment. He isn't here and he isn't scheduled to work until another shift. I can leave a message or I can let you speak to the Fire Chief....."

"Where does he live?" she barks. "Where does Caleb live in this town?"

"I can't tell you that. It's confidential information. We aren't allowed to give out the firehouse staff's personal details." I wave toward the stairs. "I think I better get the Fire Chief for you. He'll be able to explain this to you...."

She huffs in exasperation, rolls her eyes, and turns away. That's when I see her car parked at the curb outside the firehouse. She must have driven here and parked there. I didn't hear her drive up while I was in the locker room.

Another thread of fire burns my insides. Caleb is married and has a son. I don't know if I believe that bullshit story about him losing his memory. Maybe he made it all up so he could ditch his wife and disappear.

Now he's up here pretending to play house with me.

I wait until the woman gets into her car, buckles her son into the back seat, and starts the motor. Then I pull out my phone and snap a picture of the two of them.

I'm going to confront that lying, backstabbing, traitorous bastard with the evidence just as soon as I lay eyes on him again.

How dare he do this to me?! How dare he play the knight in shining armor when he's really an underhanded, manipulative cheater in disguise?

I'm shaking too badly from rage to go back upstairs to the breakroom. I need to calm down before I see any of my crewmates.

I go back into the locker room and lean against the lockers trying to steady myself. I have to force myself to breathe. I need to think.

That boy must be about seven or eight. Caleb has been working at Howe Firehouse for about that long, so the stories add up.

As soon as I calm down, a bunch of other details come back to haunt me—not about the woman's story, but about mine.

Caleb.....He immediately backed off when he found out I had a fiancé. Then he flat turned me down and refused to go out with me at all when things fell apart between me and Clay.

Caleb could have gotten me then. He could have stepped in and swept me off my feet.

Everyone at the firehouse respects Caleb. He's one of the most honorable, level-headed men I've ever met.

As far as any of them has mentioned to me, he's been single for as long as he's been working here. That doesn't sound like a man who ditched his wife and son so he could go be single in another town.

He and I have been down a long, hard road to get where we are.

If I go off on him about this, I'll be doing exactly the same thing to him that Clay did to me.

There was nothing going on between me and Caleb, but Clay completely flew off the handle and refused to consider that he might be misreading the situation.

As soon as I think that, I calm down immediately. I don't know what's going on here, but I'm going to find out. I have to find out.

Caleb might be cheating on his wife and abandoning his son.

There might be some other perfectly logical explanation for this—an explanation that jives with everything I already know about Caleb. This sure as hell doesn't.

I take a few more steadying breaths. I have to handle this rationally—and I have to give Caleb a chance to explain. I have to find out the truth—whatever it is.

I stuff my phone into my pocket and run back up the stairs three at a time. I skip the breakroom and go straight to Duke's office.

I barge in without knocking, but fortunately, the door is partially open so I'm not completely crossing the line.

He looks up. "Hey!" he greets me.

"I need to leave the firehouse," I blurt out. "I can't explain why. Something just came up. It's important. I need to handle it—just for a little while—and I'll be back as soon as humanly possible.....Call it....an extended lunch break. It's really important."

He blinks at me and then relaxes in his chair. "Okay. You can take an extended lunch break."

I spin away. "Thank you so much!"

I race back to the garage, barrel out to my car, and skid out onto the road. I don't know what's going on, but I'm going to get to the bottom of this one way or the other.

Chapter 29: Caleb

I take a deep breath and walk into the Howe County Jail. The guard at the entrance desk just told me Clay Wescott is still here.

I should be happy about it. If he wasn't here, I would have to drive all the way upstate on my next day off to see him and explain all of this to him.

He won't be able to do anything to me or Allison ever again. I just have to face him with the truth. I can't let him go to prison thinking I'm a decent guy without at least being honest with him.

The guards let me into the visitation room. I get there first and sit down at the desk.

I'm wearing my casual clothes, but all the guards here know me. The fire crew has attended way too many medical calls in the jail.

The other people visitors all sit around waiting, too. It takes a long time for the guards to bring the prisoners in.

When they do, Clay slumps in the chair in front of me. He doesn't react to my presence.

"Hey," I greet him. "You okay?"

He shrugs. "I'm all right. What's going on? Why are you here?"

I take a deep breath. "I came to tell you Allison and I are together now. I wanted you to hear it from me before you go upstate. We don't want to keep any secrets from you."

He looks away. "You deserve each other. You especially deserve her. You're the best thing for her. I hope you're happy together."

"Do you need anything?" I ask. "I don't want to hold onto the past. It was a messed-up time all around. We'll all be better off if we put it behind us. I don't want any bad blood between us. If you need anything—I'd like to consider you a friend."

He glances up at me. His eyes look haunted and tormented. "Would you mind....just leaving? Seeing you....it really hurts."

I wince. "I'm sorry, man. I didn't mean to make it worse for you."

He turns his eyes away. "Looking at you only reminds me of everything I did wrong. Being in here is bad enough without that. I have to move on, too. I can't do that if you and Allison keep visiting. Just move on and leave me alone to move on in my own way."

"All right, man. I'm sorry. I won't come again."

I start to turn away.

"Caleb!" he calls out. I turn back. "Thank you.....again......for eve rything....."

"I mean it. If you need anything, we're just a phone call away."

I walk out of the jail, but I have to stop outside, lean against the wall, and catch my breath. I'm not as nervous as I thought I would be, but damn! Poor guy. I feel for him.

I finally calm myself down and go back to my truck. I have another seven hours to run errands and do chores around the house before I have to go on shift at the firehouse.

I drive home planning on how to fix up the house, now that Allison is living there. I wish we had more time to talk about what changes she wants or needs me to make to the place. Maybe she doesn't want me to make any.

I have a laundry list of jobs I've been procrastinating on. I mentally organize them by priority on my way home.

I'm just starting to get really excited about living with her. This is going to be great—and she said she wants to start a family. I can't wait.

My heart stops when I pull into the driveway and see her car parked in the driveway. She shouldn't be home from work—at all.

She's rostered at the firehouse for the rest of the day. She shouldn't have left it until I went on shift. I shouldn't be seeing her until we pass each other in the locker room.

I park my truck behind her car. Should I be mad or worried that she's here?

I walk in and find her sitting on the living room couch. She couldn't make it more obvious that she's waiting for me.

"Hey, baby," I begin in as calm a voice as I can muster. "What's going on? What are you doing home?"

She looks up at me and takes a deep breath. This must be serious.

"I was at the firehouse just now when a woman showed up with her young son. She claimed to be your wife and that the boy was your son."

My jaw drops. "Um....what?"

"Do you mind explaining to me why you're asking me to move in with you when you have a wife and son in another city?"

I shake the stars out of my head and try to think straight. "I...I don't have a wife...or a son! I have never been married....and I never had a kid!" I flounder in confusion for a second before my head shoots up. "Wait a minute. You aren't saying you actually believe this, do you?"

She raises both hands and gets to her feet. "I'm just trying to get to the bottom of this." She comes toward me and holds out her phone so I can see the screen. "That's them."

I stare at a picture of a woman and a boy sitting in a car. "I have never laid eyes on those people in my life. You have to believe me."

"She said you got into an accident in Crayton, lost your memory, and wandered off. She says that's how you wound up in Howe."

I gape at her in disbelief. Then, without thinking, I burst out in laughter, but only for a second. This is deadly serious. This is nothing to laugh at.

I straighten my expression. "Then that proves it. I've never been to Crayton in my life, either. I was born and raised in Whitley. I moved here ten years ago after I got out of high school. I can prove it. You can ask Duke to show you my employment records. I was in a youth search and rescue squad in Howe before I went through the Fire Academy—also in Whitley. I've been working here ever since. I can also prove that I lived in Whitley for the rest of my time on this planet. I have never set foot in Crayton and I have definitely never been married there."

She studies me extra closely before her shoulders relax. "Okay. I believe you, but we need to figure this thing out. This woman is out there announcing to the world that she's your wife and that she has a son with you."

"I have no idea what this is about, but I swear to you that she's lying." I hear my voice shaking. "You have to believe me!"

She lowers her voice. "I do believe you. It's going to be all right." She comes toward me and puts her arms around me. "We're going to work this out. Don't worry."

I'm just about to collapse in relief that she actually believes me, but right then, we hear a car door slam outside.

Allison and I both turn around to see the same woman parking her car behind my truck. "Lying bitch!" I snarl.

"Stay calm," Allison murmurs in my ear. "This is a perfect opportunity to find out what she knows. Invite her in so we can talk to her."

My blood starts to boil when the woman takes her son out of the car and brings him up to the porch. I open the door before she gets here.

Her eyes don't register a single flicker of recognition when she sees me. Neither do the boy's.

She grips him by the shoulders and steers him in front of her. He stares at me in blank, white-faced horror. Maybe the man they think is his father was a really abusive asshole...so why are they mistaking me for him?

I try to smile at both of them. "Come on in," tell the mother. "I'm glad you came by."

"We aren't staying here, Caleb," the woman tells me. "We're going home to Crayton where we belong—and you're coming with us. That's all there is to it."

I wave at the living room behind me. "Please....come in. We can talk about this and work it all out."

The woman marches the boy inside. I don't even know their names.

I shut the door. "Can I get either of you anything?" I ask.

"You can come outside, get in the car, and drive back to Crayton," the woman snaps. "We've been searching for you everywhere. We're all sick and tired of this game of hide-and-seek. You're coming home—now—today."

I raise my hands. Allison's presence helps to steady my nerves, but only slightly.

"Would you mind telling me your names?" I ask. "I'm really sorry, but I don't remember either of you. I'm Caleb—but you already knew that. This is Allison Metcalfe. She's a paramedic with the Fire Department. You met her a little while ago."

The woman gives Allison a dirty look. "What are you doing here, you tramp? You better not be making a move on my husband."

Allison opens her mouth, but I interrupt. "You were going to tell me your names. Maybe that will jog my memory."

"It's Josephine," the woman barks. "And this is Benny."

I do my best to smile at both of them. "Well, it's very nice to meet you, but as I was just telling Allison, I have no memory of ever being married or having a son. I lived in Whitley all my life before I moved to Howe....."

"You don't remember because you lost your memory," Josephine fires back. "You got in a car accident and disappeared on us."

"When was that?" Allison asks. "I'm assuming it was after Benny was born."

Josephine wrinkles her nose at Allison. "It was four years ago—so you better not have been sleeping with him during that time."

"I've been working at the Howe Firehouse for seven years," I tell her. "I lived in Howe for three years before that. My presence here is well documented in the Fire Department records."

She spins around and glares at me. "Don't think you're going to weasel out of this. You can't run off with a tramp like that and abandon us." She waves at Allison. "You have responsibilities, Caleb. You're coming back to Crayton with us."

Allison takes another step forward. Benny stays glued to his mother the whole time—or she makes sure he stays glued to her. She doesn't let go of him for a second.

"Would you mind showing us some pictures of your husband?" Allison asks. "Could you show us some pictures of you and Caleb together—to prove that he really is your husband?"

Josephine bumps Benny's shoulder. The boy attacks his pants pocket and brings out a stack of crumpled photographs.

Josephine yanks them out of his hands and shoves them at me. "There. You can see the truth right in front of your eyes. Now you don't have any excuse to spin me these ridiculous lies."

I turn the stack of photographs around so I can see them. Allison comes over to me and looks at them over my shoulder.

The first one shows Josephine standing in front of a pale blue house with a man and a young boy. The boy looks like he's about four or five, but the boy in the picture isn't Benny.

The man in the picture definitely isn't me, either. He's tall, bony, has straight, shoulder-length surfer-blonde hair, and he wears glasses.

He also has extremely crooked teeth, a narrow, bony horse-face, and a massive overbite. The boy resembles his father with light-colored hair, the same narrow features, and a mouth that is way too small for his large teeth.

Josephine looks much younger, prettier, and much happier in the picture. All three of them smile and wave at the camera.

I flip through the rest of the pictures, but none of them are of me.

"None of these pictures are of Caleb," Allison points out. "There must be some mistake."

Josephine turns on her in a rage. "Shut your mouth, you filthy bitch! Don't you think I recognize Caleb when I see him?! You stole him from me, you tramp!"

Before I can even open my mouth to intervene, Josephine pulls a gun from under her dress and levels the gun at Allison's head.

Chapter 30:
Caleb

Don't ask me where Josephine concealed the gun. My one thought is that she was using Benny's body to conceal the gun behind him where Allison and I wouldn't see it.

Josephine pushes the boy out of the way. The last two shootings definitely made an impression on me.

Allison dives out of the way and I charge Josephine from the side. I take a page from Keith's book, shove the gun up into the air, and strap my body around hers so she can't lower her arm.

My weight hits hers and we topple hard onto the floor. She roars in pain when I pin her down, but she turns out to be stronger than I expected.

She rears off the floor in a blinding rage, bellows at me, and throws me onto my back. She scrambles on top of me and tries to bring the gun forward to aim at me this time.

I lunge for her arm and grab her by the wrist. How can such a frail, fleshless woman could be so strong?

She almost manages to point the gun at my head. I have to use all my strength to stop her.

She bares her teeth in feral madness, dives for the gun, and uses her other hand to drag it a little closer to my face.

At that moment, something smashes down on top of her from behind. It shatters over her head and she collapses on top of me.

I stare up at Benny standing over me with the top half of one of my dining room chairs still clutched in his white-knuckle fists.

I gasp for air and stare up at him in shock. "You okay?" I choke. "Are you okay?"

He bursts into sobs. "She kidnapped me! My name isn't Benny! It's Michael—Michael Portsmouth! She kidnapped me and threatened to kill me if I didn't pretend to be her son! I just want to go home! I want my mom and dad!"

I scramble out from under Josephine's body. She weighs nothing now.

I grab the boy in a hug. "You're okay now, Michael! You're going to be okay! We're going to send you home! You're safe now!"

I have to tug what's left of the chair out of his hands so I can hug him. I pick him up and hold him while he cries his eyes out. Poor kid.

Allison stands across the room talking loud and fast into her phone.

"Allison is calling the Police," I tell Michael. "You're going home. It's over."

He won't stop bawling in my ear, so I just hold him and pet the back of his head to keep him calm. What a nightmare.

I walk out to the garage, get a length of rope, and carry it back to the living room. I put Michael down while I tie up Josephine and kick the gun out of her reach.

I tie her up a lot tighter than I probably need to, but I don't care.

Allison hangs up, comes over to us, and kneels down in front of Michael. "Are you okay? Did she hurt you anywhere?"

He's still crying too hard to answer. He just shakes his head.

As soon as I finish tying up Josephine, the three of us sit down on the couch to wait for the Police to show up. Michael calms down and Allison gives him a sandwich and a glass of water.

It doesn't take long before the Police invade the house and take statements from all three of us. They also don't take long before they contact Michael's parents.

They live in Crayton and have to drive four hours up here to get him. Allison calls Duke to explain why neither of us will be returning to work today. The attending Police officers also confirm the situation for him.

She puts it on speaker so we can hear him. "Holy shit!" he mutters into the phone. "Can everyone stop shooting at everyone else—just for a little while?"

"This is the last time," I tell him. "I promise."

"It better be. Just make sure you two come back to work tomorrow—without any injuries or gunshot wounds."

"We will," Allison replies. "Thank you again."

We hang up and convince the Police to let Michael stay here until his parents show up instead of the officers taking him to the Police station.

They leave two officers with us just to make sure the handover goes smoothly.

We get a call from Police Chief Jim Walker two hours later. "We matched Josephine's fingerprints and found out who the man and boy in the pictures are. It turns out she was married to man named Caleb and had a son named Benny. They both got killed in a car accident four years ago. We found a trail of incidents leading all the way back to Crayton. She's been searching for her husband ever since. She kidnapped Michael to act as her surrogate son to play into the delusion."

Mr. and Mrs. Portsmouth don't pull into the driveway until almost eight o'clock at night. I open the door for them.

I don't even get a chance to invite them inside before Michael charges across the room. "MOM!! DAD!!" he yells and hurtles into his father's arms.

His father grabs him in a huge hug and both parents burst into tears. Michael starts crying again, too.

"My boy!" Mr. Portsmouth chokes. "My precious boy!"

His wife hugs both of them and sobs into her husband's shoulder. I can't help but smile as I watch them from a distance. This moment makes the whole disastrous incident worthwhile.

Allison appears at my side and slips her arm around my waist from behind. I bend over and kiss her hair. She's beyond precious to me.

My whole being overflows with gratitude that she believed me. She didn't go off on me for betraying her. She actually listened and helped me deal with this situation.

Kissing her hair doesn't satisfy me. I wrap my arms around her and hug her against me. I am never going to let this woman go—not ever.

She hugs me back. In a minute, the Portsmouths come over to me shaking my hand and then hugging both me and Allison. The two parents and Michael won't stop crying through the whole thing.

They thank us profusely and clasp my hand again and again. Michael hugs me around the waist sobbing his eyes out.

"Hey, buddy!" I push him back and kneel in front of him so he can see me. "I'm the one who should be thanking you. You saved my life. You're the hero here, not me. Okay? You did great. I'm so proud of you—and so is everyone else. Your parents are proud of you. You're gonna grow up to be something special. I know it."

I hug him again. It takes a long time to get the family out of the house before they finally put Michael in the car and drive off into the night.

Then the officers take their leave and I turn to Allison. We're finally alone.

We fall into each other's arms and I bury myself in her softness. She's still wearing her uniform. She looks the way she did that first day when I met her—but nothing will ever be the same.

"Thank you," I husk in her ear. "Thank you so much for believing me."

Her hand flies to my hair and she hugs me tighter. "I'm just so glad I still have you. I couldn't lose you. I love you more than anything."

I shut my eyes against her neck. This woman is my treasure. Everything I've ever done has been leading me to this moment. "Marry me," I husk under my breath. "Don't ever leave."

She sniffs in my ear. "I'll never leave you. I'll marry you and give you children and grow old with you. We're going to have a long, happy life together."

I kiss her, but not even that seems enough. I lead her into the bedroom, topple onto the bed, and pull her down on top of me. I need her as close to me as possible. I can never lose her no matter what.

End of Book 8.

Keep Reading

F<u>irehouse Blues Series: Book 9: Forgotten Love</u>

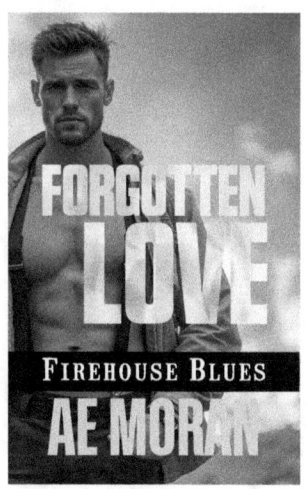

Firefighter Ellis Barret used to be the life of Howe Firehouse and everyone's favorite jokester. He's also sweet on paramedic Jessie Nash, but their friendship is too innocent to progress any further.

All of that comes to a screeching halt after Fire Chief John Brewer's tragic murder. Now Ellis won't talk to or even look at anyone, not even when Jessie tries her hardest to bring him out of his depression.

The world flips again when a serious car accident wipes Ellis's memory of the past year. His lively personality and sense of humor come back with a vengeance—and so does his desire to make Jessie his own—but is this really the real Ellis? Did the accident cause some damage to his personality that is making him act so radically out of character?

How can Jessie even believe that Ellis's love is real when he could switch back to his old silent ways and push her away tomorrow? Could the firehouse be about to lose one of its greatest heroes—just when circumstances conspire to give Ellis and Jessie the life of their dreams?

You can find it at your favorite book retailer.

Get All of AE Moran's Free Books

S ign Up Once—Get all A.E. Moran's free books including brand new releases

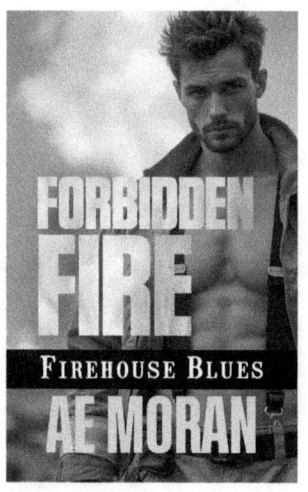

When what you want most is the one thing you can never have......

Austin McAuliffe is every woman's dream firefighter—young, strong, drop-dead hot, and selflessly dedicated to his career—and to the woman of his heart, Emma Brady. Only one other person holds a place in Austin's life—his best friend and fellow firefighter, Theo Gough. Austin insists on Theo spending time with Austin and Emma as a couple, especially when these two firefighters have a hard day at the office.

No one can believe when Austin completely flips out and randomly accuses Theo and Emma of flirting with each other in front of the whole fire crew. Could there be some deeper, more sinister reason for Austin to suddenly lose his mind and lash out at those closest to him?

Emma is devastated when Austin coldly dumps her with no warning and disappears out of her life, but Austin casts a long shadow. The nightmare of his sudden betrayal will come back to haunt Emma and Theo long after Austin is gone. Will the ghosts of the past ruin any chance for them to regain their happiness.....or will Austin's madness take down everyone he cares about along with him?

Sign up at www.authoraemoran.com to read it for free.

About AE Moran

A .E Moran is the contemporary romance pen name for Theo Mann.

I write 70 books per year—and yes, before you ask, all these books are my original creative work. Nothing written under my name is AI-generated or ghostwritten because I write better than AI and any ghostwriter out there.

People don't read fiction for entertainment or to escape from reality. People read fiction to see their humanity reflected in another person's character and story.

This is my promise to you. When you read my books, you'll see your own humanity reflected in the characters and stories. I take this commitment to my readers very seriously. My books are an intimate form of communication between us. I would never disrespect my readers by turning that over to a machine or another writer. This is my bond between me and you as my reader.

I write 20,000 words per day as my daily work output. If anyone with a public platform would like to challenge me to prove this in a controlled environment, feel free to contact me on this website's contact page.

I worked as a professional ghostwriter for fifteen years. Now I'm going for the Guinness World Record by writing 700 books over the next ten years and 1400 books over the next twenty years, all originally written by me. See my website for the full book list.

I'm also the author of *Proof for the Existence of God* and the *Crimes Against Fiction* blog. You can find all my nonfiction work at www.crimes-against-fiction.com.

If you have a story idea, or if you would like me to explore a series in more depth, or if you'd like me to explore a character by writing a spinoff series about that character or world, leave me a message on my website's contact page. I answer all reader emails, so ask me anything, tell me what you liked and didn't like, and let me know where you'd like your favorite series to go. I would love to hear your ideas and find out what you'd like to read next.

You can find out more at www.theomann.com or at www.authoraemoran.com.

Also by AE Moran (so far)